Protecting Fable

Stone Knight's MC
Book 6

Megan Fall

Protecting Fable

Published by Megan Fall

Dedication

To my family

You put up with my ups and downs, and my good and bad days. I love you all!

Contents

Chapter 1
Tripp

Detective Tripp Jamison sat at the bar with a whiskey in his hand. It was the third time this week he had been in this same spot. He had always loved being a cop, but lately it was losing its appeal. He hated doing things by the book, and over the last month, he had turned a blind eye to some of the things that had happened in town.

The Stone Knight's was one of those things. Since the captain had assigned him to a case that had involved them, he found that maybe their way was better. When one of the biker's women had been kidnapped and sealed in a mine, he had reported that one of the suspects got away. Of course, he knew for a fact that the bikers had taken care of that problem. He had even handed the man over to them.

Then another biker's woman had an ex that was terrorizing her. He knew for a fact the bikers had blown up the house the man had been staying in, but again he kept quiet. The club protected their own, so when the cops couldn't find the ex, the bikers took matters into their own hands.

Tripp also hated paperwork, and he hated taking orders, two things a detective had to do daily. Things had to be done by the book. If the bikers hadn't taken over in both those cases, the women would have died. He hated to admit it, but he was getting sick of being a cop.

"What's the matter?" his partner Darren Macks asked him. "Someone piss in your beer?"

"Fuck off," Tripp told him angrily. "I'm just trying to get some things clear in my head," he huffed. Darren's demeanour instantly changed to concern.

"You good?" he asked with a raised brow.

"Not sure," Tripp answered as honestly as he could. Then he pushed away from the bar and headed for the door. He didn't feel bad at all about leaving his partner to drink on his own. He was the type of man that wouldn't be alone long. As Tripp pushed through the exit, he saw a redhead heading in Darren's direction. He shook his head and headed for his bike.

No one knew Tripp rode but Darren. It was frowned upon at work. Detectives were supposed to be the pillars of society, and the captain wanted them all to wear suits, and ride in nice cars. Tripp hated suits, and he hated cars more. He tried to follow the captain's rules, but sometimes he needed the freedom of his Harley.

He cranked the throttle and headed for Lisa's place. Lisa was his on again, off again girlfriend. Right now, they were together, but he knew it wouldn't be long before she pissed him off again, and he left. These days, she was always doing things to piss him off.

Tripp didn't want anything serious, and so their relationship worked just fine for him. He was twenty-five and was in no hurry to settle down. Lisa however, wanted a ring on her finger and a cookie cutter house. She whined every time he blew her off and threatened to find someone else. The thing was, Tripp didn't care, and that only infuriated her more.

He pulled up in front of her house and dropped the kickstand. Within minutes he was at the door, and she was greeting him with a kiss. He pushed her inside and kicked the door shut behind him. He needed something to take the edge off, and she was it.

Two hours later, he was walking back out, with Lisa following him and begging him to stay. He refused, knowing the first time he did, he might as well move right in. That would definitely seal his fate, and he wanted no part of that.

He cranked his Harley and headed to his place, at the far end of town. It was small, but he liked it that way. He pulled into the attached garage and headed inside. Things were quiet, just the way he preferred them. He grabbed a beer out of his fridge and headed for the shower.

Ten minutes later, Tripp was done his shower, and the beer was gone. He towelled off and grabbed a pair of boxers, then lay back on his bed. He crossed his arms under his head and stared at the ceiling. He never used to be this way. He once had a life he liked, and a girl he loved.

Of course, nothing lasts forever. The girl ended up being the start of his downfall, and he couldn't help blaming her for everything that happened after.

Chapter 2
Tripp

Tripp met Fable in high school. They dated for three years, and they were just two years apart. They stayed together while he attended the police academy and continued on when he became a cadet. Once his probation was over, he proposed. She happily accepted.

Tripp had been over the moon. Fable was stunning. She was a tiny thing, with long blond hair, and the prettiest blue eyes he'd ever seen. She was fun, outgoing, and she loved to laugh. They went everywhere together, and Tripp was head over heals in love with her.

Two months after he proposed, Fable's mother got married. Fable's father had died in a mining accident years before. Part of the mine caved in, and it killed six miners. It was so bad; the mine had closed.

Fable's mother later married a businessman from Florida. He was traveling and fell in love with the town, along with her. After they married, he moved in, bringing his son Gabe with him. Gabe was the same age as him. Tripp got along with him fine, but there was just something about him that Tripp didn't like.

The wedding planning was going well, and it was eight months away. Fable seemed over the moon. She had her dress picked out already, and they had decided on the venue. There was a botanical garden nearby that was perfect, and they agreed to having the wedding and reception there.

One month later, things changed. Fable's stepfather decided it was better for his business to move back to Florida. So, he and her mother packed up and moved away. That left Fable alone in the house with her stepbrother, who had stayed. Things were fine for a month, and then they weren't.

Fable came to him one day in tears, telling him how she had fallen in love with her stepbrother, and couldn't marry him anymore. At first Tripp thought she was kidding, but as the days went by, he discovered she wasn't. The wedding was canceled, and she refused to see him.

Tripp tried frequently to see her, but her stepbrother wouldn't let him in the door. Three weeks later, his best friend was murdered. They found his body floating in the lake, with a gunshot wound to the head. Kevin and him had been best friends since kindergarten. He was supposed to be Tripp's best man at his wedding.

It devastated Tripp. He attended the funeral in a daze. First, the person who was supposed to spend the rest of her life with him, left him. Then, his best friend was murdered. Tripp pushed everyone else away and gave up on Fable. It was obvious she had moved on, and he needed to do that as well.

And that's where Lisa came in. She had gone to high school with them, and was always trying to get together with him, not caring that he was with Fable. He was in a bar one night, drowning his sorrows in alcohol, when she approached. This time, he didn't say no, and that's how she became his on again off again girlfriend. He didn't care about her, and hell, he didn't even like her, but that made it all easier.

Fast forward to now, and he was in a job he hated, dating a woman he hated. The only light in his life was The Stone Knight's. They could always be counted on to stir up shit, and they kept things interesting. If it wasn't for them, he had no idea how he would ever cope with things.

He still saw Fable occasionally around town, but he avoided her, and she ignored him. She had distanced herself from everyone but her stepbrother, and she pretty much stopped going out. Fable dressed differently too, preferring stylish things, to the almost entirely gypsy wardrobe she had when he was with her. She wore her hair up and covered her face in makeup.

Some days he missed his pretty little gypsy girl, but those days were gone, and they were never coming back. Now he only felt anger towards her, and he couldn't stand the sight of her.

Chapter 3
Fable

Fable walked down the street with her head down. The high heels her stepbrother Gabe insisted she wear, were killing her feet. The dress she wore was modest, but uncomfortable, and she felt like a stepford wife in it. She hated what he made her wear.

When Fable was in high school, she discovered a love for vintage clothing. Tripp used to call her his gypsy girl, and she loved it. Her mother took her to a secondhand store. She found several skirts there, both long and short, in a flowery soft material, and her wardrobe just grew from there. She had off the shoulder loose blouses, embroidered jean jackets, high boots, glittery flip flops and bell-bottom jeans.

When Gabe first came around, he refused to call her Fable, saying it was a name for a no good hippy. He now called her Fay, and she hated it. Her dad had named her Fable, and it was one of the few things she had left of him. He had died when she was little, in a mine cave in, and she missed him terribly. She had been daddy's little girl, and he told her how much he loved her every day.

When her mother had remarried, she had been thrilled to get a stepfather and stepbrother. She had always wanted a big family, and she had one now. They seemed to love Tripp and were looking forward to her wedding. But not long after that, things changed. Her stepfather moved back to Florida and took her mother with him. Unfortunately, Gabe stayed.

Gabe just seemed to snap one day. He took all her clothes and burned them in a fire in the backyard. Then he presented her with bags of things he deemed appropriate for her to wear. Next, he was rude to all her friends, and eventually drove them away.

Fable had been terrified and threatened to tell Tripp. At the time, he had just gotten on the police force, and he was going through the training to become a detective. Fable had been so proud of him. Gabe had pulled a gun and threatened to kill Tripp unless she broke up with him.

She refused to put Tripp at risk, and broke up with him right away. She knew he had a temper, but he had crushed her heart when he believed the garbage she was spewing, and stormed off. That day broke her. Loosing Tripp was devastating. She gave into Gabe, and wore the clothes he picked out, and acted the way he wanted.

A couple weeks later, she had been crying at the park, when Tripp's best friend, Kevin, had found her. She had desperately told him what was going on, and he had been furious. Kevin had hugged her and kissed her head, then told her not to worry, because he'd fix everything. The next day, they found his body floating in the lake. Someone had shot him in the head, execution style. She never tried to talk to anybody again. Gabe now had an army of men working for him, and that made him even more dangerous. She had no idea what he did for a living, but she knew it was bad.

Fable looked up for just a minute and found herself staring into a pair of familiar eyes across the street. Tripp stared back, but his stare was full of fury and disgust. She couldn't help it, a couple tears fell and rolled down her cheeks.

While she watched, Tripp's eyes zeroed in on them, then he frowned. She didn't wait to see what he would do, she turned and hurried in the other direction. It had been two years, so she didn't know if Gabe's threat still stood, but she wasn't taking any chances. She hurried home and headed upstairs to her room. Once she was inside, she locked her door and threw herself on her bed.

Maybe she should just disappear. She couldn't live with Gabe anymore because it was destroying her. And, she couldn't stand the way Tripp now looked at her, that destroyed her more.

Chapter 4
Tripp

Tripp stood on the sidewalk and waited for the light to change. When he glanced up, he froze, as he locked eyes with Fable. She looked ridiculous. Her hair was pulled up into a tight bun, she wore a pantsuit with a high-collared blouse underneath, and her heels were unbelievably high. She looked like the exact opposite of the girl he used to love.

His lips turned up in a sneer, and he couldn't hide his disgust. Every time he looked at her, he remembered the day she broke his heart. As he watched, a tear rolled down her cheek, and she turned a deathly shade of white.

He tilted his head as he studied her, then watched as she turned and hurried back down the street, in the direction she had obviously just come from. He watched her go in complete confusion. They rarely saw each other, so she had surprised him today.

He didn't understand why she had paled and cried. Every other time he had seen her, she had quickly looked the other way. He knew Gabe was into some shady stuff, but the department had nothing they could pin on him. The guy appeared squeaky clean on paper, and that pissed all the cops off.

Maybe it was time Tripp used some of his connections and looked into Gabe himself, off the record. He knew if he went by the letter of the law, he wouldn't get anywhere, but he could if he did it his way. He had no idea if Fable was into the business side of things, but he couldn't stand by any longer. If she got hurt, so be it. She made her own bed, she'd have to lie in it.

The first call he made was to Mario. Mario was a member of The Stone Knight's, but he ran his illegal business on his own. It rang three times before it was answered.

"Why in the fuck are you calling me?" Mario growled at him. Mario was a great guy, but he was a criminal. The only time Tripp had dealt with him, outside of work, was at Trike's wedding.

"I need information," Tripp told him. "It's for personal reasons," he added. "Can we meet?"

Mario was silent for a while. "Meet me at the strip club in ten," he ordered. Then he hung up, effectively ending the call.

Tripp sighed. He hated the strip club, and even though it was closed at this hour in the day, he cringed at the thought of stepping in there. Mario's strip club had blown up a while back, but the man had rebuilt it. He strode back to where he parked his truck and climbed in. A few minutes later, he was pulling into the parking lot of the club.

Tripp headed inside and blinked at how bright it was. Usually he was here on a call, and the club was open. The lights were low, the alcohol was flowing, and the patrons were rowdy. He headed into the main part of the club, and it was eerily silent. A glance around, and he spotted Mario sitting at the bar. He had a drink in his hand and was surrounded by paperwork. Mario looked up as he approached and glared at him.

"If this is a setup, I'll kill you without even blinking," he threatened.

"First of all, don't threaten to kill a cop," Tripp advised the man.

"Who the fuck are you gonna tell if you're dead?" Mario returned with a small smirk. Tripp conveniently ignored him.

"Second of all, I'm off the books," Tripp explained, as he pulled out his badge and gun and laid them on the bar in front of him. Mario just raised a brow at him in surprise.

"I'm not a cop right now," Tripp informed him. Mario studied him a minute, then nodded.

"I hear you have a habit of not completely doing your job anyway, and The Stone Knight's like you, which says a lot. I loved watching you look the other way after we dug Misty out of the mine. I have to say, you don't make a very good cop though," Mario chuckled.

Instead of arguing, Tripp just nodded. "Yeah, I'm thinking that myself," he admitted. Then he watched as Mario reached over the bar, snagged a bottle of whiskey and another glass, and set them down. After pouring two shots, he turned back to him, and handed him one.

"Drink up, then we'll talk," Mario ordered.

Tripp did just that. He left the club a lot later with a fuzzy head, but he had a lot of information he hadn't had before. He ignored his truck, deciding to walk instead. Now he needed to sober up a bit before he headed to The Stone Knight's compound, because he had a feeling he'd be drunk again later.

Chapter 5
Tripp

After about three hours, Tripp was pretty sure he was sober enough to walk back to his car. God damned Mario had gotten him drunker than he thought. He was back at the strip club ten minutes later, but it was open now, so he avoided it like the plague. After climbing into his car, he started it up, and headed toward The Stone Knight's compound.

Fifteen minutes later, he was pulling up at the gate. Dagger was there and came strolling over when he saw him.

"Detective Jamison," he greeted, as he tried to peer inside the window. "What brings you to this neck of the woods today?"

"Relax, its personal reasons today," Tripp told the biker. "I need information on someone, and I was hoping the club could help me out."

Dagger studied him a minute, then nodded. He reached for his cell and put it up to his ear. "The good detectives headed your way. Hide the guns and dynamite," then Dagger chuckled as he hung up.

Tripp could only frown at the biker.

"They said to give them a minute," Dagger relayed with a straight face.

"Bunch of clowns," Tripp mumbled, as he pulled through the gate, but he did it with a smirk on his face. He parked at the end of all the bikes, then walked back to the door. Once there, Steele stepped out.

"This private, or can we talk at a table in the common room?" the biker asked.

"Nah, it's just info I need, common rooms fine. But I've already been to see Mario today, so go easy on the liquor," Tripp complained.

Steele just snickered, as he led the way to a table where Dragon, Trike and Navaho sat.

"Detective Jamison," Dragon smirked. "What brings you to our neck of the woods?" Tripp sat down, then stared at the biker.

"You fuckers rehearse this shit," Tripp asked him. Then he shook his head and proceeded to ask them about Gabe. Of course, drinking ensued, and Tripp ended up drunk again.

"Fucker stole my girl," Tripp slurred about an hour later. "I was gonna marry my gypsy, then he walks in, and she falls for him. Next thing I know, the weddings off. Broke my heart she did." By this time, Ali and Cassie had joined them and were sitting on their men's laps.

"She doesn't love him," Cassie informed him, shaking her head. It took Tripp a minute for that to sink in, then he blinked.

"She does," he told her.

"Doesn't," Cassie immediately responded.

"Does," Tripp responded with a glare aimed at her.

"She doesn't," Cassie pushed, glaring right back. "Open your damn eyes," she sneered. Then she leaned over and smacked him in the back of the head. Chuckles were let loose around the table.

"My ex husband abused me," Cassie admitted. "And I can recognize the signs." Steele growled and pulled her close. "That girl cringes when he touches her, and he never touches her intimately. She hates what's she's wearing, and she doesn't say boo to anyone anymore."

Tripp blinked at her again, trying to clear the alcohol from his system. "What?" he questioned, as he sat there stunned.

"She's curling in on herself. Keeps quiet, keeps her head down, and hopes he doesn't notice her. It's what I used to do," Cassie admitted.

"Fuck me," Tripp roared. Then he thought of something and turned back to Cassie. "Why doesn't she ask me for help?"

Cassie dropped her head. Then looked straight at Steele. "She doesn't want you hurt," she whispered. Steele roared, then stood, taking Cassie with him.

"You're done here Little Mouse," he huffed. "Catch you brothers later," Steele said, as he kicked open the door and carried her out.

"That's how you get your way with your girls?" Tripp asked. "Just carry them away, and you win." The men just chuckled again, but Ali looked furious.

"That's not how it works," she snickered. But then she squealed as Dragon picked her up and carried her out too.

"Huh," Tripp slurred in shock. "That definitely works." Then he turned to Navaho and saw two of him. "I'm drunk again, aren't I?" he asked the biker.

"Sure are," Navaho responded. "Let's get you to a room so you can sleep it off."

And that's what he did, passing out as soon as his head hit the pillows.

Chapter 6
Fable

Fable was getting worried. Gabe was furious about something, and he was taking it out on her. She knew it was business related, but she wished he would just move on and leave her alone. He was yelling at her more too. She had to change three times this morning before he allowed her to leave the house, and he was scowling at her all the time.

But the worst thing happened yesterday. Fable had walked into his office, delivering a package, and he had been yelling on the phone. Apparently, his men had seen her and Tripp staring at each other across the street. They never followed her, she had just been unlucky that day. Even though Gabe knew she had turned and fled when she saw Tripp, he was furious with her.

Fable had screamed, when he had grabbed a knife from his boot, and sliced her palm. It wasn't too deep, but she knew she'd probably need stitches. She had cried as he had ordered her to stay away from Tripp. Then he had explained that Tripp was a cop, and he didn't want any cops around him.

When Fable had tried to tell him she needed stitches he waved her off, telling her not to let a doctor near her, or he'd cut her again. She had hurried away and cleaned it as best she could. She had to wrap it quite a bit before the blood stopped seeping through.

Fable now knew the reason he had made her break up with Tripp. She had no idea why she hadn't realized it sooner. With Tripp just getting on as a detective, and with Gabe doing so many illegal things, it all made sense. Plus, he had said the words more cops. That meant they were looking into him now and was most likely the reason for his bad mood lately.

Fable headed to the store later that day, hoping to find something she could make for dinner. As she walked down the street, she could feel eyes on her.

She stopped and looked around, freezing when she saw Tripp leaning against a lamp post across the street. This time he was staring at her as if he was studying her, and it unnerved her. The other day he looked surprised to see her, but this time, the surprise wasn't there.

Quickly Fable dropped her head to face the sidewalk once more, then hurried faster in the direction of the store. When she pushed the door open, and walked inside, she let out a sigh of relief. She had no idea what Gabe would do if he found out she had seen Tripp again. Even the distance between them didn't seem to matter anymore.

Fable grabbed a small basket and hurried down the isles. She rushed to pick out a small roast, fresh bread, some baby carrots, and a couple baking potatoes. She was hurrying to the cash, when Tripp came around the corner from the opposite direction. She stopped just in time before she crashed into him.

"Tripp," Fable whispered, as she stared up at him. He looked like he was about to say something, but she turned and ran the other way. Without seeing him again, she paid for her things, and left the store. She thanked god she had worn a long-sleeved sweater today, because when she tugged the sleeve, it completely covered her bandaged hand.

She hurried down the sidewalk, heading home once more, but when she passed the lamp post again, she looked up. Once more, Tripp was leaning against it as he watched her. She stumbled slightly in surprise, and she saw Tripp stand up straight, almost like he was concerned, but again she caught herself and looked away. She refused to turn back as she practically ran the rest of the way home.

What the hell was going on with him, she thought. She'd seen him more today than she had in the two years since she broke up with him. But she vowed to try harder to stay away, she'd lose the last piece of herself that she was trying to hold on to, if anything happened to Tripp.

Chapter 7
Tripp

Tripp leaned against the side of a car as he watched Fable walking down the other side of the street. Luckily, she hadn't noticed him yet, because every time she did, she ran away. He was beginning to detect what Cassie had told him. Fable always looked so unhappy, she kept her head down, and she was quiet. If someone tried to talk to her, she brushed them aside, and continued walking.

She looked incredibly uncomfortable in the clothing she was wearing, something else Cassie had pointed out. She walked stiffly, and she kept pulling at the high collar of her blouse. The poor girl looked miserable.

"Who are we looking at?" came a voice from beside him. Startled, he jumped about a foot. When he turned, Trike was standing beside him.

"Jesus," Tripp growled. "For a big guy, you're fucking quiet." Trike ignored him as he stared at Fable, who had stopped to peer in a vintage shop window. Now that was his gypsy, Tripp thought to himself. He tried to see what had caught her eye, but she was too far away.

"That your girl?" Trike questioned, as he propped himself on the car beside him.

Tripp frowned at the biker. "Do you mind?" he demanded. Again, Trike ignored him.

"Girl dresses weird," Trike frowned. "My grandma dresses better than her." All Tripp could do was huff at the man. "You gonna go talk to her?" Trike challenged.

"I need to figure out what's going on first," Tripp told Trike. "I can't risk her getting hurt by charging over there. I need to know what I'm up against."

"You got a message or a trinket you can give her?" Trike pushed.

"Why?" Tripp responded.

"She needs something to show you haven't forgotten her. Something that isn't personalized, so nobody but her knows it's from you."

Tripp thought for a minute, then he reached into his pocket and pulled out his keys. On his key chain was a miniature metal feather. Fable had given it to him when they had first dated. He had kept it as a reminder of how she had hurt him. He removed it and held it out for Trike.

"I'll be back in a minute", the biker declared. Then he watched as Trike crossed the street and casually bumped into Fable. If he wasn't watching so closely, he would have missed Trike slip the small feather into her hand. It looked like Trike was apologizing, then he was moving away, and headed back across the street.

Trike leaned against the car beside him once more, and the two of them watched as she opened her hand to see what was in it. It looked like she gasped, then she searched all around, probably struggling to find him. Tripp knew she couldn't see him where he was positioned. She gave up and glanced back down at her hand. Then her fingers folded around the trinket, forming a fist, and she brought it to rest against her chest.

Tripp frowned, as once more she turned and practically ran down the street. Her reaction though had sealed the deal. She had treasured the trinket and held tight to it, that meant it still meant something to her. Tripp was more determined than ever to get to the bottom of things. If Gabe was hurting her, he was gonna find out.

"You want to watch her?" Trike asked, interrupting his thoughts. "You get out that motorcycle you're hiding, dress in your leathers, and wear a helmet with a face mask. I guarantee nobody will know who you are."

Tripp stared at the biker in shock. "How the hell do you know about that?" he demanded. Trike just looked back at him like he had two heads.

"You think you're so sneaky," Trike chuckled. "Just because it's dark, it doesn't mean we can't see you dumb ass," he stated. Then the biker turned and strode away.

"Well shit," Tripp mumbled. Then he turned too and walked away. He had a lot to do, and he was ready to start moving ahead with things.

Chapter 8
Fable

Fable was confused. She had absolutely no idea what was up with Tripp. For a week solid the man had been everywhere, and he was constantly watching her. For two years she had had little to no contact with him, now she was seeing him every day. But he never approached or tried to make contact, he calmly studied her, and it was unnerving.

Then a couple days ago, a biker from The Stone Knight's had bumped into her and slipped something in her hand. She would have thought it was an accident, but when she peered down, she recognized the little metal feather.

When Tripp was accepted into the police academy and had to go away for training, she had given him the key chain. She had been deathly afraid that he'd meet someone else, so she gave him the trinket so he'd remember her. She had been a gypsy girl back then, and she loved feathers, so she felt the trinket was appropriate.

Back then, Tripp called her Gypsy, and she adored it. It broke her to say goodbye to him, and she had made sure he despised her, which was why he was unsettling her now. She had been successful; she knew it by the distain he repeatedly showed her.

Now there was a motorcycle following her. It would appear out of nowhere, stop close to her, then speed off. The driver wore a full-face mask, so she had no idea what he looked like. He didn't wear a vest, so she knew he wasn't part of the motorcycle club, although she had seen him with them.

She wasn't afraid of the motorcycle man though. He almost comforted her with his presence. It was like he was checking up on her, and once he was certain she was fine, he'd take off. She hadn't seen Tripp over the last couple days, so the bikers appearance was welcoming.

Today Gabe was on edge because he had a meeting with Mario, and the man was about to arrive. Gabe wanted to get in on some of Mario's business, because he wasn't getting far on his own. Although what business, Fable had no idea.

When the doorbell sounded, she answered it dutifully, and let Mario in. She had strict instructions to bring him straight to Gabe's office. She spun to lead the way when Mario seized her hand. Immediately she cried out, as it was the one with the knife wound. She drew her hand back and cradled it with the other one. No one had noticed it yet, as she always pulled her sleeve over it. Even the biker hadn't noticed, since he put the feather in her other hand.

"What the fuck?" Mario growled, as he grabbed her hand once more. She struggled to pull away, but he held firm as he studied the bandage that had blood on it. Without stitches, it wasn't healing well, and she knew it was a touch infected.

"Did he do this?" Mario demanded, as he nodded towards Gabe's office.

"Please," Fable begged as she glanced around. It wouldn't go over well if someone caught them.

"Prepare yourself," Mario told her. "Tripp will hear about this, and he'll come for you," he swore. "Little birds are whispering in his ear," he added softly. "And the good detectives listening." Then he kissed the back of her hand, and let her go, continuing on his own to Gabe's office.

Fable stood there dumbfounded, not knowing what to do, until Gabe bellowed her name. She scurried to his office, fearing the worst, and shoved open the door.

"Mario's having a party at his house tonight, and we've just been invited. I want you dressed and ready by seven," Gabe ordered. Fable let out the breath she'd been holding and exhaled in relief.

"Of course," Fable answered, and turned fleeing the room. What the hell was Mario up to, she thought. And since when was a criminal in cahoots with a cop. Things were growing complicated quickly, and she prayed Tripp stayed away. Gabe was losing it fast, and she didn't want Tripp to get caught in the fallout.

Chapter 9
Tripp

Tripp was getting ready for the party. Mario told him it was casual, so he was content to don his jeans. He knew it would be a lot of businessmen, but a few of The Stone Knight's boys would be there. That actually made Tripp breathe easier. He was ready, and he was heading for his keys when the doorbell rang. He glanced at it in annoyance, wishing to be on his way.

When he opened it, it confused him to see Lisa standing there. She had on a long trench coat and was smiling at him seductively.

"Hey baby," Lisa purred. "I come baring gifts," she declared, as she opened the coat to display the black teddy she was wearing underneath. Tripp frowned down at her. Honestly, in the week he had been following Fable around, he had completely forgotten about her.

"We're done," he informed her, as he pulled the door shut and locked it behind him. "Go home, find a man who appreciates you," Tripp ordered. She looked aghast as she watched him lock up.

"But we always break up, and you always come back," Lisa whined, as she tried to rub up against him.

"Lisa, no," he urged, as he gently forced her back. Suddenly, she put her hands on her hips and scowled at him.

"Who is she?" she angrily sneered.

"Who's who?" Tripp questioned, as he headed to his car. She was right on his heels.

"You've met someone. Who is she?"

"Lisa, this is ridiculous. Now I'm late, and you need to leave," Tripp told her. He was on the edge of loosing his patience.

"I'll find out who she is," Lisa threatened, as he climbed in his car. "You and me, we're good together. She can't replace me," she shrieked, as he closed the door.

Tripp shook his head at her as he backed out of the drive. He would have to keep and eye on her. She had always been so easy going. This was a side of her he'd never experienced before. He glanced in his rear-view mirror, to see she was still standing there, watching him drive away. He turned his attention back to the road and put her out of his mind. He needed to be on his game tonight, and she was a distraction he didn't need.

Mario had set this party up, so he could speak to Fable. Tripp had been watching her for a week, and was pissed to see that everyone around her had been right. He had no idea why he didn't see it before. It must have been because he was hurting, he had let his anger rule his head. He had a lot of work to do to fix all this, but he would do it.

Mario had surprised him yesterday, by dropping by for a visit. He mentioned he had something he needed to tell him in person. When Mario had told him about the injury on her hand, he had lost it. Tripp now had to replace his kitchen table, and two of his chairs. Mario had calmly explained that was why he told him at his house, the ass.

Tripp had called Steele, and suggested that Doc attend, with his medical bag. He wanted her hand looked at. Steele had agreed, but now he, Dragon and Sniper were attending too. The women were being left at the compound as the men didn't want either of them getting in Gabe's crosshairs.

Tripp pulled through the gate and parked at the side of the house. He was happy to see the bikes parked there, that meant the club members were already inside. He breathed deeply, then greeted one of Mario's men at the door and headed in.

The house was packed with men in jeans and shirts, and woman in cocktail dresses. Tripp was stunned to see so many people, as Mario had set this up in just a day. He owed Mario big time.

He scanned the room, not seeing Mario, or Fable and Gabe. But he eyed Steele and the boys, so he headed that way. He couldn't wait to get a hold of Fable, but he needed to keep his head in the game. Things were gonna move fast tonight, and he was impatient to get back his girl.

Chapter 10
Fable

Fable stood at Gabe's side and hated every minute. The dress he made her wear was horrible. It was black, tight and boring. It fell to her knees; it had a high round neck and long sleeves. Luckily, with the long sleeves, she added a black scarf to her wrist and wrapped it around her hand, hiding her injury. Gabe had screamed at her for that, but when she took it off, the bandage was so white, it almost glowed against the dress. He was pissed, but he told her to put it back on. Her hair was once again in a fancy twist, and her heels were high, and plain black.

The party was in full swing when they arrived, and the house was full. Fable was extremely nervous around people, and she was instantly uneasy, as all eyes turned to them. Thankfully, Mario appeared out of thin air and moved to their side.

"Gabe, so glad you could make it. I want to introduce you to some people, and then we can talk in my office for a bit," Mario greeted smoothly. He glanced at her and smiled, then made his way through the crowd.

Mario stopped at about four other men throughout the next hour, but Fable just looked at her feet and ignored them. Finally, Mario was done, and he told them it was time to talk. When Gabe roughly grabbed her arm, and pulled her with them, Mario stopped.

"I'm sorry," Mario apologized. "I will only discuss my business with you. I don't allow outside ears to hear, and I assume you don't want her to know your business either."

Gabe frowned at the man. "I don't, but I'm not comfortable leaving her alone," he disputed.

Mario nodded and waved someone over. A huge biker stepped to her side. She stared up at him in fascination until Mario drew her attention.

"This is Steele, he's one of The Stone Knight's. I promise she'll be in good hands while we talk. He won't let anyone close, and he has a beautiful woman waiting for him at home," Mario reasoned.

Gabe nodded, then leaned in close. "Be good, if not, you'll have a matching wound somewhere else on your pretty little body," he sneered. Then he pulled away, and smiled at Mario, following the man away. She stood there, pale and a little frightened.

"You okay?" Steele asked quietly.

"No," Fable answered, then blinked, and hurried to change it to yes, but he was already narrowing his eyes at her.

"Let's fix that," Steele growled.

Then with a gentle touch, he took her arm and led her through the crowd. It surprised her when he opened the doors to a room at the end of a small hall and gently nudged her inside. She turned to watch, as he shut the doors behind her, not stepping inside. The room was dimly lit, and she was frightened once more.

"You know," she heard from a very familiar voice off in the corner. "I fell hard once for this pretty little gypsy girl, but she ended up destroying me. She decided she loved someone else, and she left me. I wanted a life with her." He paused then.

"God," he growled, "she was my world, my heart and soul. Unfortunately, I let anger rule my actions, and I took her at her word, and walked away."

She had no idea what to say, so she stayed silent and still as he continued.

"I was a stupid, angry, dumb ass, and I didn't listen to the words carefully. You see, my pretty little gypsy loved me as much as I loved her. She was a mess when she told me, but I didn't care. I never realized she didn't mean a word she was spewing, and it was breaking her, to say such nonsense. I walked away and never looked back."

She sucked in a huge breath, trying to keep the sob from coming out. She was terrified he would hear it.

"I'm not dumb anymore, and my eyes are wide open. My gypsy needed me, and I turned my back on her. I'm not going to fucking do that again," he said, and this time his voice came from right in front of her. "You're mine," he growled. "Always was, and always will be."

She backed up, but her back hit the door. Tripp was saying everything she wanted to hear, but it would mean his death.

"It's too late," Fable whispered, as she broke once again.

"No, it's fucking not," Tripp roared. Then she was pulled into his strong, warm arms, and his smell was enveloping her.

Chapter 11
Tripp

Tripp had Fable in his arms, and he was fucking thrilled. It had been so long, he'd forgotten what she felt like. It was her, but it wasn't her, and he hated that. He knew she was gonna fight him, and he was preparing for that. But right now, he had to fix one tiny thing.

"Kick off your shoes Gypsy," Tripp ordered. When she only stared up at him, he sighed. "My Gypsy's short as fuck, and those heels are horrible." Immediately, the shoes disappeared, and she dropped a foot. "Better," he stated.

Then he leaned over, flicked a switch on the wall, and it flooded the room with light. She blinked up at him as he looked her over. She looked horrible again. The dress was atrocious, the hair made her look like a librarian, and the makeup hid her pretty face. He hated it, but he didn't say a thing.

Carefully, he moved her aside, and opened the door. Immediately Doc walked inside, wearing jeans, a shirt, and his cut, and in his hand was his medical bag. Steele was still there playing sentry, and he closed the door once Doc was through. Fable eyed the doctor skeptically, then moved closer to him.

He immediately pulled her in tighter, then took her injured hand in his own. She panicked and pulled at it, but he didn't let go. Gently, he started to unwrapped the scarf.

"Tripp no," Fable cried, as she continued to pull at her hand. "Please," she said, as tears streamed down her face.

It killed him to ignore her, but he did, as the scarf floated to the floor. He gazed at the bandage and was horrified to see the blood. Furiously, he picked her up and carried her to the couch. He sat, so she was on his lap, then motioned for Doc to move over.

"You can't do this," his Gypsy pleaded. "Gabe doesn't want a doctor to look at it. You have to let me go."

"Hold still honey," Doc ordered. "This bandage is stuck, and I don't want to hurt you." She slumped and placed her head on Tripp's shoulder. Tripp held her arm still on her lap as Doc got to work. She cried out once, then the bandage was gone.

"God damn it," Tripp roared, as got a look at the wound. It was red, pussy, and bleeding, and he didn't need to be a doctor to know it was infected.

Doc didn't say a word as he inspected it, then he unloaded supplies beside him. He picked up a needle and pulled the protective cover off it.

"This will numb the area. I need to clean it well and stitch it. I can use invisible thread, that way no one can see it," Doc explained. Then he nodded for Tripp to hold her, and he inserted the needle. She cried out and shoved her face in Tripp's neck.

A few minutes later, Doc got to work. He poured a shit ton of antibiotics on it, then stitched it up. He covered it in a cream, then wrapped a clean bandage around it. Next, he pulled out another needle, and before she could protest, pushed up her dress and shoved it in her thigh.

"That was a high dose of penicillin," Doc explained. "That infection's bad." Then he packed up his things and walked out.

"He made a mistake when he touched you," Tripp told her. "You're staying with me now," he ordered.

She caught him by surprise when she slipped off his lap and moved away, picking up her scarf, and slipping on her shoes.

"I'm not staying with you," Fable told him, as she swiped at the tears. "I'm leaving here with Gabe." Then she cringed as she tied the black scarf around the bandage to hide it once more.

"You fucking are," Tripp growled at her.

"I want to say yes," Fable cried. "But I can't. You're a cop, you find a way to take him down, and you do it quickly," Fable whispered. "I can't tell you why, but I can't leave him right now. You do what you should have done before. You get me out of there, but you do it legally."

Then she turned on her heels, straightened her shoulders, and pushed out the door. Tripp headed after her, but Steele stopped him.

"The meeting just ended. Gabe's looking for her. Now is not the time brother," he ordered. Then Steele prowled after her, presumably to deliver her back to Gabe.

Tripp glared at the man's back, then turned on his heel and started pacing. He had to find something on Gabe, and he had to find it fast.

Chapter 12
Fable

Fable hurried after Steele, as he headed for Gabe. Her stepbrother was standing with Mario, and his head was twisting right and left as he searched for her. When he saw her, he marched towards her, and grabbed her arm. She cried out as his grip tightened, and looked up at him, but Mario's growl caught her attention. Both him and Steele had moved up beside her.

"Let her go," Mario calmly ordered Gabe. His face revealed his anger, but his voice was completely controlled. "You want to work with me, there's something you should know. I don't condone hurting women, if I find out you do, our dealings will be immediately severed. Do I make myself clear?"

Gabe quickly loosened his grip. "Understood," he responded in a clipped tone. "But Fay's my stepsister, and sometimes she needs reminding of appropriate attitude and appearance, as her status warrants."

"That may be true, but sometimes you need to let a woman fly. It's amazing how beautiful they can be when they're not caged," Mario pushed.

"I'm not sure I agree," Gabe countered. "But I won't hurt her. If you don't mind, I'd like to get her home."

Mario nodded. "I understand." Then the men shook hands, and Mario turned to her. When he leaned in, he kissed her cheek, and whispered in her ear. "Believe in Tripp."

Then Steele was leaning in to do the same. "Tripp has all of us," he whispered. "And now, so do you." He kissed her cheek and leaned back. Then stated loudly to Gabe. "Fable hung in the library while you were gone, didn't seem comfortable in the crowd."

Gabe seemed to relax slightly hearing that. "Thank you for taking care of her." Steele nodded back.

Then Gabe turned and pulled her after him. Fable twisted to find the two men watching her. She mouthed thank you, and held her hand up in a half wave, then watched as they both smiled sadly at her. She had no idea how a cop could have men such as them as friends, but she couldn't be happier. They were wonderful, and she loved that they were backing him up.

The ride back to the house was quiet, and Fable had a lot to think about. She was shocked over Tripp's about face in his attitude towards her, but it was a relief to know he was seeing the truth about things. But Gabe had killed his best friend when he tried to help her, so she was terrified of that happening to him. That was why she wanted him to do this legally. Then hopefully Gabe would be behind bars where he wouldn't be able to hurt Tripp. They pulled up to the house, and she got out, following him inside.

"I think that went well," Gabe smirked. "But you need to learn how to shut your mouth. If I want to hurt you I will, and those two aren't gonna stop me. Any pain I inflict on you, needs to be hidden. If it blows back on me, you'll end up at the bottom of the river with a bullet in your head, just like that piece of shit that tried to stop me before."

Terrified, she could only nod. "Get up to your room," Gabe ordered. "I'm sick of looking at you." Then he turned and headed for his office, and she turned and headed up to her room. Once inside, she stripped and threw the clothes in a pile in the corner. Then she slipped on her rainbow baby doll nightie, one of the few things she truly loved. Gabe never came in her room at night, so it was safe to wear it.

She flopped on her bed and stared at the ceiling. Tonight, for the first time in a long time, she had hope. It was a nice feeling to fall asleep with.

Chapter 13
Tripp

It had been a week since Mario's party, and Tripp wasn't getting anywhere. He and his partner Darren were going through every file they had on Gabe and were coming up dry. This was why the police couldn't prosecute the man. He had all his illegal activities buried deep, almost like he was hiding them in a vault.

They managed to take down three of his guys though, but they hadn't given up their boss, and Gabe just turned around and replaced them. Tripp knew he was getting to the man. Gabe had to feel the pressure, he just hoped the man didn't take out his frustrations on Fable.

Mario was also pissing Gabe off. After the party, he knew Gabe assumed he was in, but Mario just kept putting him off. The man had no intention of working with Gabe; he was just providing an opportunity for Tripp to get his girl alone for a few minutes. Tripp was extremely grateful to Mario, but Mario just waved him off, saying that's what friends do.

Tripp was pissed too, about Fables hand. The cut had been nasty and it was infected. That was something that Tripp didn't want to happen again. Once was bad enough, but a second time would absolutely blow his mind.

He slammed his fists down on his desk in frustration and yanked at the tie they forced him to wear. He was losing his patience, all because the guy looked squeaky clean on paper.

"We'll get him partner," Darren promised. "The man will make a mistake, and we'll be there to bring him down," he tried to assure him.

"The fuckers been in this town for two years, and we got fuck all. If we get a warrant, he knows it's coming, if he has a deal going down, he sends one of his lackeys. I'm sick of it. If we go in guns blazing, we'd find something, and we'd have him," Tripp sneered. "But this job makes it impossible to do that."

"Right, and if we do that, chances are he'd turn it around, and we'd be the ones going down. We have to do this by the book, it's the only way," his partner pushed. Then he rubbed his chin and titled his head. "Maybe we're looking at this the wrong way," Darren continued. "What if we investigate your girl?"

"You better explain yourself fucker," Tripp growled.

"Why is she still with him? Why not just walk out? And why does he want her with him? It's obvious he doesn't like her, so why keep her around," Darren questioned.

Tripp thought about it for a minute. "You got a valid point," he conceded. Then he picked up the phone and put it to his ear.

"Who the fuck are you calling?" his partner asked.

"The Calvary," Tripp told him. When Steele answered, he told him what him and his partner had come up with, and asked for his help. The brother immediately said he'd get on it and promised to see what Mario could find out as well. Tripp hung up, knowing between The Stone Knight's and Mario, things would get done.

Four hours later, they were back to square one. Neither he, nor Darren could find anything on Fable themselves that would explain why Gabe was so interested in her. He hoped Steele had better luck. He was furious and on edge when he packed up, getting ready to head out for the day.

Just as he was leaving, his captain called him and his partner into his office. After fifteen minutes of yelling, the captain dropped the bomb that they were to cease all further investigations on Gabe. The man was filing a harassment suit against the department, and the captain was beyond angry.

When he threatened to suspend Tripp and Darren, Tripp lost it. He pulled out his service revolver and slammed it on the desk, then he unclipped his badge from his belt, and slammed that down as well. When his captain asked what the fuck he was doing, Tripp was more than happy to explain.

"My girls shacked up with a guy that sliced her hand for shits and giggles. The man is buried so deep in illegal activities it isn't funny, but what does this department do?" Tripp practically growled. "Nothing but suspend the cop investigating the asshole, and let the asshole continue on doing the fucked up shit he's doing. Now if that isn't whacked, then I don't know what is," he sneered.

"I'm done with this shit job. You can take your suspension and shove it up your ass. I quit," Tripp roared, then he turned and slammed out the door.

Chapter 14
Fable

Fable ducked, as a glass came flying out of the office and smashed against the wall beside her. Gabe was losing it. Lately, he had no control. He yelled, he threw things; he fired his men and then he rehired them the next day.

She tried to sneak past the open door, but knew she wasn't successful when he called out her name. She sighed, and was scared to death, as she slowly made her way to him. He sat behind the desk, glaring at her as she approached.

"The fucking cops are breathing down my god damned neck," Gabe roared. "They were persistent before, but now it's like they're making it their mission to take me down. I had to fucking go in there with a lawyer, and threaten to sue the whole place to get them to back down," he told her.

She couldn't stop the shaking in her hands as she listened to him. If he managed to get them to stop the investigation, then Tripp didn't stand a chance of finding anything on him. And, if Tripp found nothing, it would be hard for her to get away from him. She needed him behind bars.

The doorbell rang interrupting him, and he waved his arms, dismissing her so she could answer it. Thankful to have an excuse to leave him, she hurried to the front door. When she opened it, it surprised her to see one of her neighbours there. Mrs. Clark lived across the street and had three children, one of which was resting in her arms right now.

"Fable honey," she said. "I thought you should know that Mrs. Johnson had a heart attack last night." Mrs. Johnson was another neighbour, and one that used to babysit her when her mother had to work. The lady had to be in her late sixties now.

"Oh my god," Fable cried. "Is she okay?" she quickly questioned.

"I heard she isn't doing too well. They have taken her to the hospital, and I knew you'd want to go visit her. She doesn't have much family," Mrs. Clark informed her, which was something Fable already knew.

"Of course, thank you so much for telling me," Fable replied. Mrs. Clark gave her the room information, then left. Fable shut the door and hurried back to Gabe. She was near tears when she entered his office. He looked up when he heard her enter.

"What the fucks the matter with you?" Gabe huffed in annoyance. She explained about Mrs. Johnson and told him she wanted to head to the hospital right away. With the way he was acting these days, she wasn't sure he'd allow it.

"You want permission to go see her?" Gabe repeated in disbelief. She nodded her head at him in confusion when he smiled cruelty at her. "Come here," he demanded.

When she was near, he pulled her tight against his chest, and looked down at her. She'd never been this close to him before and was suddenly terrified.

"You can go, I'll even have one of my men take you, and wait for you outside," Gabe promised her. She relaxed, and then she felt a burning pain up her side. She looked down to see he had his knife out once more, and had sliced a deep cut up her entire side. It started just above her hip and stopped right at her bra. Her blood dripped from the blade. Fable screamed, as an immense amount of pain set in.

Gabe laughed as he pushed her away, and she stumbled. "Now you have a reason to go to the hospital," he sneered at her. "But again, you better just see that old bat, and not get any help. If I find out you saw a doctor, I'll put a bullet in your head," he threatened once more. "My driver will be out front in ten minutes, clean yourself up, cover that cut, and change your clothes."

Fable ran crying from the room. Things just escalated, and she had no idea what to do.

Chapter 15
Tripp

Tripp sat in the compound, drinking a beer and talking with Sniper and Dragon. He had just finished explaining everything that had happened since Mario's party. During his explanation, Steele, Shadow and Trike had joined them. He told them about her hand, he told them about his investigation, and he told them about quitting.

"So, you're coming over to the dark side?" Dragon asked with a smirk.

Tripp sighed. "The legal way got me fucking nowhere," he complained. "My girls stuck there, taking his abuse, and I don't fucking know why. She asked me to put him behind bars, but that's not gonna happen." Tripp slammed his hand down on the bar. "He sued the god damned department to get me off his back. What the fuck am I supposed to do now?" he complained.

Steele turned to him with a serious look on his face. "You do it the biker way. You grab your girl, you make her fucking safe, and you smother her with all the support and love you fucking have to give," he ordered.

Tripp turned to him stunned. "What?"

"Women think they can fix things on their own," Dragon snickered. "They fucking deal with psychos, and think they have a chance, afraid to bother us with their problems or ask for help. You gotta step in and fucking take over. Look at Ali and Cassie. They went through shit before we waded in," he explained.

Dagger came walking up then. "So, we get to use the dynamite again," he grinned.

Tripp frowned at the biker. "Is that your fix for everything?" he questioned.

"Hey, don't knock something that works," Dagger replied. "You want me to hook you up?"

"I'll let you know," Tripp promised him, not dismissing the idea yet.

"You helped this club big time," Preacher admitted as he joined them. "You've saved our asses on several occasions. You turn dark, you go all the way," he pushed, as he threw a vest down on the table in front of him. "You've been a part of this club for a hell of a long time, you just never had the vest to make it official. You're not a cop anymore, it's time to be a biker," he ordered.

Tripp picked up the vest and studied it. It didn't have a prospect patch on it, it was a vest for a fully patched member. Tripp stared at his name on it in stunned silence.

"You can't be serious?" Tripp said with quite a bit of surprise. "Isn't that like cheating, getting a full patch while everyone else has to prospect?"

"We took a vote," Steele announced. "You're in."

"I'm in," Tripp repeated. Then he picked the vest up and put it on. "I'm fucking in," he roared. "Let's go get my girl, and let's do it the biker way."

The brothers all roared in excitement, and gave hearty congratulations. Tripp was over the moon. He finally felt like his life was heading in the right direction. He was worried Raid and Sniper would be pissed, but the prospects smiled, and seemed genuinely happy for him.

Beers were handed out, but all eyes turned to the door as Misty came barreling in. Trike and Sniper stood up as they caught the tears in her eyes. Trike opened his arms, and she ran right into them. Then she turned to her brother.

"Do you remember Mrs. Johnson?" Misty asked him.

"You mean that old lady who lived next door to us for a while?" Trike questioned.

"Yep, where we lived just before the accident," Misty replied. "She had a heart attack last night, and she's not doing well. I want to go to the hospital and see her. She was so sweet to us."

Tripp looked at them in confusion. "You lived beside Mrs. Johnson?" he questioned.

"Yep, but not for long," Sniper responded. "Why?"

"Because my girl lives beside Mrs. Johnson," Tripp told them.

Misty's eyes suddenly lit up. "Fable," she squealed. "Your girl's Fable. You have to come to the hospital with us, she loved Mrs. Johnson, and I'd bet dollars she'll be there."

Preacher turned to the group then. "Well lets go visit Mrs. Johnson," he ordered.

Tripp watched as every biker in hearing distance stood and headed for the door. He grinned as he followed them, thinking he was gonna love being a biker.

Chapter 16
Fable

Fable stumbled to the bathroom and shut the door. She carefully pulled off her blouse and studied the wound. It was fairly deep and long, and she had no idea how to cover it. She pulled out a ton of gauze and medical tape. She piled on the gauze as best she could and used the tape to secure it.

It was bleeding badly, and she knew the blood would soak through. She picked up a small black hand towel and placed it over the area. Next, she grabbed two of her expensive scarves, and wrapped them around her stomach to hold the towel in place.

She knew she only had a minute left, so she didn't clean off the blood from her side, only washed her hands. Then she hurried into her closet and pulled out a long black skirt that had an elastic waist, and a burgundy shirt that was made of a soft jersey material. She hoped it was loose enough so it hid the towel, and dark enough to hide any blood.

After slipping on her heels, she hurried to grab her purse, and headed outside. Gabe's driver was there waiting, along with one of his men. He opened the door for her, and she carefully climbed inside. Her side screamed at the movement, and she prayed the bandages held.

Ten minutes later, they pulled up to the hospital. Fable got out and was shocked to see Gabe's man follow her inside. They both got in the elevator and headed up to third floor. When they got off, Fable looked for room six, finding it almost right away. Gabe's man pointed out a waiting room down the hall and ordered her to get him when she was done. If she didn't find him in an hour, he would find her. All she could do was nod, as she pushed open the door, and headed in the room.

Mrs. Johnson was sitting up in bed, surrounded by pillows. Fable hurried over, and kissed the lady's cheek, noticing how pale she was. She looked like she had aged ten years in a week. Fable sat in the chair beside the bed, and Mrs. Johnson regaled her with tales of her ride in the ambulance, and how handsome the older doctor was that was attending her.

Twenty minutes into her visit, it startled her when the door opened. She twisted in her seat, biting her cheek from the pain, and looked towards the door. Her mouth dropped open when Misty and her brother Noah walked in. They lived next door to her for about six months, before the accident that took their parents life, and left Misty blind.

She got along well with Misty, and they were the same age. Unfortunately, Gabe found out about the new friendship and stopped it before it even started. Then Misty moved away, and her brother was sent to fight in Afghanistan.

Fable stood and held on to the arm of the chair for support. Her side was hurting more and more, and she was trying not to pass out. Misty approached, and was heading in for a hug, when Fable put up her hand to stop her. She knew the hug would send her screaming, so she stopped it.

"I've got a bit of a cold," Fable told her old friend. "I don't want you to catch it."

Misty didn't seem to care and launched into how excited she was to see her. Then without taking a breath, she hurried to the door and threw it open, explaining that they brought friends.

Fable's mouth dropped open, when six large bikers walked in. She recognized Steele right away and shyly smiled up at him. He smiled back at her, then nodded to the door. Again, the door opened, but this time Tripp walked in, and he was wearing a biker vest like the other men.

"Tripp," she said breathlessly, as she watched him move towards her. "What are you doing here?"

"I'm getting my girl," Tripp told her, as he wrapped his arms around her, and pulled her into his chest.

Fable couldn't help the cry that slipped past her lips, from the pain it caused. She swayed against him, just as he pulled his arm back, looking down at it. She gasped when she saw it covered in blood.

"What the ever loving fuck," Tripp roared, as he stared down at her furiously.

Chapter 17
Tripp

Tripp studied Fable as she looked at the ground. The blood on his arm terrified him, but he also noticed she was pale, trembling, and there was a sheen of sweat on her forehead.

"Is it your side?" Tripp growled as he glanced down at her. She didn't answer, but she backed up. He made sure that for every step she took back, he took one forward. Finally, her back hit the wall, and she had nowhere to go.

"Let me see?" he ordered, as he reached for her shirt. She slipped to the side, batting his hand away.

"You have to leave me alone," Fable begged him.

"That isn't going to happen Gypsy," Tripp snarled back at her. "That fucker hurt you again. Now you can show me, or I can have one of the boys hold you while I take a look," he told her. He watched as she paled even more and started crying. That probably wasn't the best thing to say, but he was pissed.

"You can't help me, nobody can help me," she sobbed.

"I can help you. That fuckers not getting near you again, I can promise you that," Tripp vowed. "I'll deal with him myself."

"No," Fable screamed. "You can't go near him, promise me you won't go near him," Fable pleaded, as she clung to his shirt. "He'll kill you. He's done it before," she whispered, then she froze and sank to the floor as she realized what she said.

Tripp stared at her in stunned silence. Gabe had actually killed someone, and Fable knew about it.

"Who did he kill Gypsy?" He growled. When he looked around the room, he noticed all the bikers had moved in closer. Fable sat on the floor sobbing.

"I have to go," she whispered. "I was only given an hour, Gabe has a man in the waiting room. He can't find me here with you", she said, obviously panicking. She tried to get up, but she screamed in pain, as she fell back down.

Shadow stepped forward. "Me and Raid will track down Doc," he advised. "We'll be back in a minute."

She cried out no, but the brothers ignored her, and left. Tripp crouched down on the floor and moved close. Then he tilted her chin, forcing her to look at him.

"Do you trust me?" He asked quietly.

"I've always trusted you," Fable admitted to him.

"Then Gypsy, tell me who he killed?" Tripp pleaded. Her crying had stopped, but tears still streamed down her face. She grabbed at his vest and looked up at him sadly.

"I was in the park crying one night. I missed you, and it was killing me. Kevin found me," she told him.

Tripp reared back, falling on his ass. "What the hell are you saying?" he demanded.

"Kevin said he'd help me. He said everything would be fine. He was found floating in the river with a bullet in his head the next day," she whispered. "So, you can't help me. He threatened to do the same thing to you."

"Like fuck," Tripp bellowed. "That little prick's a dead man. Kevin was my best god damned friend," he hissed. "He died trying to help you, while I did nothing. That shit ends now. You come home with me right the fuck now, and we fix this."

"He'll kill you," Fable repeated. Steele moved to crouch down beside them then.

"You see this patch," he asked Fable, as he pointed to Tripp's vest. When she nodded, he smiled. "It means he's a member of The Stone Knight's now, and he's got the entire club behind him. You'll come with us and stay at the clubhouse. Gabe won't get close," Steele promised. "You belong to Tripp, you belong to us now too."

"Everything's gonna be okay," Fable whispered as she looked between all the men.

"Ya Gypsy," Tripp agreed. "Everything's gonna be okay." Then he leaned down and kissed her head, and she fell into his arms.

Chapter 18
Tripp

Tripp held onto Fable as she relaxed. Finally, she was agreeing with him and letting him take control. It may be because he was wearing a vest and had a shit ton of bikers behind him, or it may be because she was so broken, she was just done. The poor girl had been through a lot, and with what she had told him about Kevin, he now understood why she did it alone.

Kevin had been his best friend, and he loved Fable like a sister. It was no surprise that he died trying to help her. He was relieved to know who had killed him. Whether Gabe had done it himself, or whether someone had pulled the trigger on his orders, Gabe would pay. He was a biker now, and doing things legally wasn't a concern anymore. Gabe would be taken care of the biker way, and Tripp would be the one to end him.

"I need to get a look at that cut Gypsy," Tripp told her. Then he leaned her back against the wall and carefully pulled her shirt up. He was madder than hell to see a towel held on with a couple ugly scarves. He undid them and slowly pulled them away. Then Misty appeared, grabbing Fable's hand, and sitting close on the opposite side. Fable leaned against her and sighed.

Doc came hurrying in next, luckily Mrs. Johnson had fallen asleep, and she was completely unaware of what was going on. Doc crouched down on Fable's other side and smiled at her.

Tripp went for the towel next, and as gently as he could, pulled it away from the wound. It was full of blood, and stuck in a few places, so he took his time. When it was off, he saw all the gauze she had tried to cover the cut in. It was covered in blood, and it looked like a mess. Doc stopped him from removing the gauze.

"We need to move her to an exam room. I can't do this on the floor, and I can already tell you she's gonna need a shit ton of stitches," Doc explained.

Tripp nodded in complete agreement, but Fable grabbed his arm.

"There's a man in the waiting room," she whispered. "He'll be coming for me soon. And there's a man at the entrance, he's Gabe's driver, and he brought us here."

Tripp watched as Steele took out his phone. "Mario," he greeted. "Need your assistance. We have two assholes at the hospital we need transport for," Steele paused for a minute then. "A van would be outstanding," another pause. "No, the men won't be breathing to care. Ten minutes works for me, appreciate it."

"Dagger, you and Navaho take care of the man in the waiting room," Steele ordered. "Me and Shadow got the one at the entrance. Tripp, go with your woman. Take Misty, Trike and Sniper with you. Fable knows Misty and Sniper, and I know Trike won't leave Misty."

Preacher nodded in agreement with everything Steele had said. "Me and Raid will go to the entrance with you and watch out for Mario. I also want to keep an eye out in case more goons show." Then he turned to Doc. "You still on shift?"

"Shift ended fifteen minutes ago. I can take care of her, then they can take my Tahoe and I'll drive Tripp's bike," Doc responded.

"Do we even want to know what you plan on doing with them?" Misty asked.

Preacher smirked. "Bad things," he said.

"Fuck brother," Trike huffed, as he glared at the prez.

Preacher ignored him. "Let's move," he said. The brothers left while Tripp picked up his Gypsy. She whimpered, but made no other sound of protest. He cradled her close, with Misty, Trike and Sniper at his back, as he followed Doc down the hall.

Doc gave her a sedative, then cleaned and stitched up her side. Tripp was pissed when he saw how deep and long the cut was. He promised then and there to make her safe, but unlike Kevin, Gabe was gonna be the one with the bullet in his head.

Chapter 19
Fable

Fable woke up slowly and knew right away she was with Tripp. She opened her eyes, surprised to see she was in a car, and Tripp was driving.

"Tripp," she whispered. "Where are we going?"

Tripp turned to face her, and she saw the concern in his gaze. "I'm taking you to the compound. It's where you'll be safest. Besides you belong with me," he growled. "How are you feeling?"

She moved slightly, and her side didn't hurt too bad. She was groggy, but she figured that would pass in time.

"Not too bad," Fable admitted. "I assume Doc gave me something for the pain?"

"Yep, and I've got more in my pocket," Tripp informed her. "You feel even a tiny bit of discomfort, you let me know." She nodded her agreement.

When she looked around, she was surprised to see motorcycles surrounded their vehicle. She recognized Steele and Noah, although she figured she should call him Sniper now, and Misty was riding on the back of a man's bike right beside her. She saw Fable watching and waved up to her, so Fable smiled and waved back.

"I didn't know you knew Misty and Sniper?" Tripp asked.

"They moved in just after we broke up. They weren't there very long before the accident happened. I'm so happy Misty got her sight back," Fable told him.

"Yep," Tripp agreed. "She had it pretty rough for a while, and she's literally gone through hell, but she has Trike now, and her brothers back for good. She's doing well."

"Good," Fable said with a small smile. "So why the biker club suddenly?" she asked. "I thought you loved being a cop?"

Tripp glanced over at her and smiled, then turned back to the road. "In the beginning I did. But the more time I've spent with the bikers, the more things I've seen to change my mind. I've watched their women get hurt time and time again, and there was nothing I could do. I'm forced to wear a suit, sit in an office, and push paperwork. Even with your situation, I couldn't do a thing," Tripp grunted, with a deep scowl on his face.

"The bikers handle things themselves. If someone hurts or threatens their woman, they take care of it. Just like now. We got you out of there, took care of his men, and got you the medical attention you needed. In a couple hours we've accomplished more than I have in years."

They were pulling up to the compound now, and she watched in fascination as the gates rolled open. Tripp drove up to a building that looked like a warehouse and parked close to the door. He jumped out and hurried to her side, throwing open her door and lifting her up. She curled up in his arms as another biker shut the door.

Tripp carried her through a door, and into a room that looked like a bar. Couches were scattered around the edges, tables were littered everywhere, and a huge bar sat off to the side. Tripp moved to one couch and sat down. He frowned down at her angrily, and she couldn't figure out what was wrong.

"I hate your hair," Tripp said with a frown on his face. "I hate your clothes, I hate your shoes, and I hate your makeup," he continued. Fable blinked up at him for a minute and looked around to see the bikers moving in. Suddenly she got angry. She assumed the bikers thought Tripp was being mean, and they didn't know she agreed with him.

Fable carefully pushed off Tripp's lap and stood on her own. Then the tears fell. "I hate them too", she cried. She kicked off the heels, not caring where they flew, and she saw one biker duck. Then she ripped at all the pins holding her hair up. Those too, she threw across the room. Then she took the sleeve of her shirt and desperately scrubbed at the makeup. When she went to lift it over her head, Tripp jumped up and stopped her.

"Not gonna fucking happen," he growled. "We'll fix the clothes in a minute in my room."

Fable realized what she had almost done and turned bright red. "Maybe I should lie down for a bit, until these pills wear off," she admitted.

"I think that's a good idea," Tripp replied as he scooped her up. The bikers roared in disappointment as he carried her from the room.

"Fuck off," he snarled to the sound of chuckling, not only the bikers, but his Gypsy's as well.

Chapter 20
Tripp

Tripp pulled his Gypsy close to his chest as he wandered down the hall. He had literally been a biker for hours, and he had no idea where he was heading. He had easily found the hall with all the bedrooms, but he didn't know which one to use.

"Keep going, second last door on your right," Preacher ordered from behind him. He glanced back, and nodded at the prez in thanks, then continued down the hall. The door was open, so he headed inside. The room was small, but comfortable looking. He headed for the queen bed on the other side of the room and laid Fable down. She was already out, so he covered her with a blanket, and kissed her head.

Tripp was worried about her side. Her hand was healing well, now that Doc had fixed it, and the infection was gone. Her side was bad though, and Doc said he'd have to keep a close eye on it. Why in the world Gabe wouldn't allow her medical attention, was beyond belief. She could have died from that cut, and he didn't think that's what Gabe wanted.

Tripp turned, as Doc and Misty entered the room. Misty was bouncing on her toes, she was so excited, and Tripp wondered what was up.

"I need to take you somewhere," Misty quietly told him. "It's really important," she added, when he looked at her and frowned.

"Go with the girl," Doc pushed. "Fable will be out for a while, and that chair in the corner looks comfortable. I'll rest here so if she wakes, she won't be alone." Then he moved further into the room and sat in the chair, leaning back and closing his eyes.

Tripp took a long look at Fable, then followed Misty, shutting the door behind him. When they left the building, Misty stopped beside Trike and Sniper.

The brothers were standing beside a huge ass four door truck. Tripp turned to Misty curiously.

"I thought you had something to show me. You didn't say anything about leaving the compound," he questioned.

"It won't take long," Sniper assured him. "I know what she's talking about, and it's fifteen minutes away. Plus, all your shit is at your house, and it's on the way too. We can grab it and be back in about an hour. You do plan to stay at the clubhouse, right?" the biker questioned.

"Of course," Tripp immediately agreed. "Let's roll," he said, as he climbed in the backseat with Trike. Sniper drove, and his sister sat up front with him. She was creeping him out, with the huge ass grin on her face, and the way she kept looking back at him in excitement.

True to his word, fifteen minutes later Sniper was pulling up to a storage facility. He entered a code and drove down the back to where the smaller units were located. He stopped in front of one, turned the truck off, and climbed out. They all followed him. He pulled a key from his pocket, unlocked the unit, and rolled up the door.

"One night, around eight I guess," Misty started. "There was a lot of yelling going on next door. Fable's mom and stepdad had already moved away, so it was just Gabe and Fable there," she continued. Tripp was listening to Misty, but he watched as Sniper moved boxes around in the unit's back.

"Me and Noah watched from the window," Misty explained. "Gabe was furious at her. He was screaming and she was crying. He was carrying boxes out to a fire pit and dumping them in. When they went inside for a bit, we snuck over and peeked in the boxes," she moved closer to Tripp then, and placed her hand on his arm.

"It was clothes Tripp, all these beautiful colourful clothes. Gabe was planning to burn all Fables clothes," Misty told him. "Well Noah had already had most of his training, and my brothers the best at what he does," she grinned proudly. "He got all those clothes to our house and filled the boxes with old clothes we planned on throwing out. Ten minutes later, Gabe dragged out Fable, and made her watch as he burned them all. That girl was devastated."

Tripp was stunned. That must have broken Fable something bad. She spent years collecting the pile of clothes she had. He had even found some things he knew she'd like and bought them for her. His heart broke for her.

"Found them," Sniper piped up from further back. Out he popped with two boxes in his arms. He set them down and went back for more. When he was done, six boxes were on the ground at Tripp's feet.

"You want your Fable back?" Trike asked, as he pounded him on the back. "Well these two just made that possible."

Tripp grinned as he stared at the boxes, then he picked Misty up, and spun her around, ignoring Trike as he yelled at him to put her down.

Chapter 21
Fable

Fable woke, to find her head pillowed on Tripp's arm. She was lying on her good side, and he was wrapped around her. She couldn't help but smile, excited to be with him once more. She never once thought she would get to be in his arms again.

She tried to move, but it pulled at her stitches, and she cried out in pain. Tripp was instantly awake and frowning down at her.

"Jesus Gypsy, don't rip those stitches," he warned. "Doc had to put in a lot, and that cut was fucking deep." He pushed her hair out of her face and kissed her forehead. "Let's get you up. You can use the bathroom to do your morning stuff, then I have a surprise for you," Tripp smirked. She looked at him curiously.

"What kind of surprise?" Fable asked.

"One that will make you really happy," Tripp replied. Then he slid out of bed and gently helped her to her feet. She was surprised at how much the movement hurt.

"I think you need some pain medicine too," Tripp declared as he studied her. She nodded, then turned away and headed for the bathroom. She was ashamed of the wounds Gabe had inflicted on her.

She didn't get far before Tripp was there, pulling her back to him. "I still know how you think Gypsy," he told her. "I know you think you were doing the right thing by protecting me, but you weren't," he admonished.

"But he killed Kevin," Fable replied, as the tears started to run down her face. Tripp looked sadly down at her.

"He did, but Kevin went about it the wrong way. I was a cop Gypsy, I had the entire force behind me. I could have at least got you away from him," he huffed. "Kevin should never have gone in alone."

"I'm so sorry I told him," Fable cried, as the tears flowed faster. He wiped them away, then cupped her cheek.

"Never be ashamed of asking for help. That's what Kevin should have done, he should have come to me," Tripp replied angrily. He held her for a while before pulling back. "Go get cleaned up, I want to see you smile."

She nodded and headed back into the bathroom. She was wearing one of Tripp's t-shirts and her underwear. She had no idea what happened to her bra or her pants, but she didn't really care. She splashed some water on her face, brushed her teeth with the toothbrush that was on the counter, and combed her hair.

Tripp was waiting for her when she stepped out. He crouched down and held out a pair of pink pyjama pants. She placed her hand on his shoulder and stepped into them. Then he slipped a pair of flip flops on her feet. Even dressed as she was, she felt more like herself than she had in a long time. Tripp then took her hand and led her to the common room.

She was shocked to see Misty, Sniper and Trike waving her over to the corner of the room. They were surrounded by boxes, and she had no idea what was going on. Sniper lifted one and set it on the table, then motioned for her to look inside. She was a bit self conscious, when she noticed all the bikers in the room had gone quiet and were watching her.

Fable made her way to the box and lifted the flap to peek inside. Not believing her eyes, she opened the flap further and dug around inside. Tears rolled down her eyes, as she peered at some of her precious clothes, clothes that Gabe had burned.

She looked at the other boxes, and immediately several bikers came over and lifted them all onto the table. Each one opened the box in front of them, then moved away. She sobbed as she saw they were all filled with her old clothing. She looked at all the bikers, then at Misty and Sniper, then finally at Tripp.

"How?" Fable whispered through her tears. Tripp moved towards her and wrapped her up in his arms.

Maybe these giant bikers were really angels from heaven she thought.

Chapter 22
Tripp

Tripp watched as his Gypsy cried over the clothes. She rooted through the boxes, and each item she found, made her smile that much bigger. She constantly alternated between hugging Misty, Sniper and himself, then going back to the clothes. The brothers looked on with grins on their faces as well. It was amazing to see a woman who was broken only moments before, so full of joy and life now.

Fable finally stopped going through the boxes and walked straight over to him. She moved so they were almost chest to chest. She had to crane her neck to look up at him, and he saw the sadness was lingering in her expression once more.

"I want to be your Gypsy again," Fable said, as she held up one of her favourite colourful scarves. He took it from her and lifted her hair as he slipped it under to lie against her neck. Then he brought both sides up, and tied it at the top, turning it into a headband. Finally, he slid the band slightly, so it placed the knot at the side of her head, and the ends of the scarf fell out of her face.

"You've always been my Gypsy," Tripp told her, as he cupped her chin. "You just got lost for a while. It's what's inside you that made you mine, not your clothes. Now you're my Gypsy again, on the outside and the inside. And I swear to god, I'm not gonna lose you again."

He leaned down then and kissed her. It started out soft, but quickly turned heated. He stopped, pulling back when the catcalls and whistling got distracting.

"Will you forgive me for being an ass?" Tripp pleaded. "I should have known the shit you were spewing was garbage. I should have saved you then," he said miserably.

"You're forgiven," Fable whispered quietly. Then she leaned against him, and he pulled her close.

"Get the god damned twinkly lights out again and the ladder," Dagger huffed. "We got another god damned wedding to decorate for," he mock complained. Everyone chuckled, and it broke the sad moment.

"Let's get these boxes to Tripp's room brothers," Preacher ordered, as he picked up one of the boxes himself. Sniper, Trike, Dagger, Dragon, Steele and Shadow each picked up a box and headed down the hall.

"Do you think we're all gonna have to go barefoot and sing lullabies at the wedding?" Dagger asked as he walked away.

"You're in charge of the harp," Steele teased him.

"I'm not fucking playing a harp," was the last thing Tripp heard, before the men were out of hearing distance.

"Oh, I'm so getting him a harp," Raid smirked, as he headed for the bar.

"I'll start breakfast," Navaho informed them, shaking his head as he headed for the kitchen.

Tripp took Fable's hand and led her back to his room. All the boxes were placed on the floor in the corner, and the brothers were already gone. Tripp left her where she was and headed for the boxes. It took him routing through three of them before he found what he was looking for. She laughed, when she saw what he held up.

Tripp had just started dating her, and it had been her birthday. He had searched every vintage shop he could and had finally found a pair of jeans he liked. They were a faded blue pair of bell bottoms. The side had an embroidered flower up the leg, and they sat low on her hips. She had loved them on sight, and had worn them so much, the bottoms were frayed and there was a hole in the knee. She hadn't cared and had just kept wearing them.

Tripp had also pulled out a soft black blouse that fell off one shoulder. He figured the blouse was loose enough, that it wouldn't rub on her side, and the jeans were low enough that they wouldn't bother it either. He smirked at her as he held out the clothes.

"Do you need help?" Tripp asked. She laughed as she smiled at him.

"I take it you're the one that put me in your shirt?" Fable questioned. He smiled and shrugged. "Then yes, I would love your help to get dressed." He grew serious as he moved towards her.

"And just so there's no confusion," Tripp growled. "We will be getting married, and I'll make all the brothers go barefoot if that's what you want." She threw her head back and laughed, and it was the prettiest laugh he'd ever heard.

Chapter 23
Fable

Fable lifted Tripp's shirt as high as she could, then stopped. She barely had her arm even with her shoulder when it pulled the stitches and hurt. She cried out and instantly let go. Tripp was by her side in a minute. He pulled her close and wrapped her up in his arms.

"You need to be careful Gypsy," he soothed. "I thought you said I could help you, you weren't supposed to start without me." Fable pulled back and smiled up at him.

"I really missed you," she whispered.

"I missed you too," he whispered back.

Then he lifted the shirt and gently helped her pull her arms out. She was embarrassed when he helped her into her bra, but he was a gentleman, and made it easy on her. He then slipped the blouse over her head and got her arms in. He picked up her jeans next and held them out. She gripped his shoulders and stepped into them, waiting while he pulled them up.

He surprised her by placing a warm soft kiss on her tummy before doing up her jeans. She closed her eyes, trying to savour the feeling. When she felt his lips on hers, she immediately kissed him back. It felt like no time at all had passed between them. When he pulled away, she still had her eyes closed, and she was breathless.

"I can't believe I forgot how pretty you looked after I kissed you," Tripp told her. She blinked a couple times and looked up at him.

"Tripp," Fable whispered breathlessly.

"And there she is," Tripp declared, with a look of pure joy on his face. "The girl of my dreams. A sweet, dreamy look on her face. My favourite outfit on her. Her hair down, but tied back from her face with a ribbon." He cocked his head and studied her. "You're missing something though," Tripp frowned.

He turned and started searching through the boxes again. When he came back, he held a wooden box. It was the jewellery box he had made her in shop class. He had even carved a stunning heart in the top with their initials inside. Tears fell from her eyes.

"I didn't see that in the boxes," Fable admitted. "I thought he threw that away."

He wiped her tears and opened the lid. He pulled out a pair of big hoop earrings and carefully put them in her ears. Then he took out her choker. It was a simple piece of black lace, with a small moon pendant hanging from it. He clipped it around her neck.

Then he reached in and pulled out a small turquoise ring. He had also given her this in high school. She knew he had worked hard for months in order to buy it. He slipped it on her engagement finger and smiled down at her.

"Now it's official," Tripp told her. "You're mine again, and we're gonna get married. No way in hell am I loosing you again."

She wrapped her arms around his waist and buried her face in his shirt. She was so happy, she thought her heart would burst. Just then her stomach growled, ruining the moment.

"Let's get my Gypsy fed," Tripp chuckled, as he took her hand. "Navaho makes a mean breakfast," he explained, as he led her to the common room. They entered the large room once again, and just like before, everyone stopped what they were doing to stare at her.

It only took a minute before whistles and clapping filled the room. Embarrassed, she ducked her head and smiled, while she clung to Tripp's hand.

"I'd like to introduce you fuckers to my fiancé, Fable," Tripp shouted over the noise. They stopped for a minute, stunned. Then the shouting got louder and the bikers all stood and charged them. Tripp ended up tackled to the ground, and Navaho came to stand guard in front of her. Anyone who got close he roared at, reminding them of her stitches.

She loved the bikers, and laughed as Tripp tried unsuccessfully to push the bikers off that were piled on top of him.

Chapter 24
Tripp

Not too long after breakfast, Tripp could see that Fable was in a lot of pain. She'd taken her pain meds, but they hadn't quite kicked in yet. She was pale and looked extremely tired. Tripp decided it was time for her to rest.

She had been sitting on his lap anyway, so he shifted her so she was facing him, and had a leg on either side of him. He placed his hands on her butt and stood. She didn't protest at all, just wrapped her arms around his neck, and rested her head on his shoulder. That was all the confirmation he needed.

When he headed across the room, Steele called out. "Preacher wants us in church in ten."

Tripp nodded and kept going. When he got to his room, he stopped cold. It looked like they had tacked giant colourful scarves to all the walls and then draped them across the ceiling. It made the room look like he was stepping into a tent. They had strung little white Christmas lights up like garland around the walls. Colourful lanterns hung from the ceiling, and a bright red shag rug covered the floor. There was a colourful tie dye quilt on his bed, and a peace sign had been spray painted on his bathroom door.

"Fucking bikers," Tripp grumbled. "I've heard stories about this crap, but I've never seen it until now."

Fable lifted her head off his shoulder and tried to twist to see. Instantly she whimpered when the movement hurt her side.

"I think the view will be better from the bed," Tripp replied sarcastically. He carried her over and laid her down. Her eyes grew wide as she tried to take everything in at once.

"What is this?" Fable inquired in awe. Tripp could only sigh.

"When one of the brothers find their one, the other brothers like to decorate their room in outrageous colours. It's kind of a right of passage now," he explained. She tilted her head and looked at him.

"The one?" Fable questioned.

"It's like a soul mate," Tripp responded, as he laid down beside her. "When a brother sees his one for the first time, it's like he stops breathing for a minute, the feeling hits him so hard. He just knows she's the one. Apparently, it feels the same way for the girl."

"And you felt that way with me?" Fable asked shyly.

"When we started dating, I already knew you, and was already half in love with you. But it felt like that the first time you talked to me, and the first time you smiled at me. I was a goner," Tripp told her.

"I felt that way too," Fable admitted, as her eyes fluttered closed. "I love the room," she whispered, then she fell asleep. Tripp kissed her forehead, pulled a light blanket over her, and left the room. A minute later, he was pushing open the doors of the room they used for church.

"Who the fuck put all that shit in my room?" Tripp roared, with a murderous expression on his face. Instantly, every brother there raised their hands.

"Thank you," Tripp replied, as he lost the look, and smiled at the brothers. "Fable loved it, and if it makes her happy, it makes me happy."

"Well fuck," Dagger huffed. "You're supposed to fucking hate it," he pouted. "You're no fun at all."

Tripp chuckled. "Sorry brother," he apologized, as he shrugged his shoulders.

"Ali kept the pink comforter the brothers gave her," Dragon piped up.

"Cassie kept the peach one too," Steele added.

"Misty kept the one we got, and the rug," Trike added.

"You fuckers suck," Dagger sneered. "When I get my woman, that shit ain't happening," he vowed.

All the brothers chuckled, knowing he would probably be the biggest sap of them all.

Chapter 25
Tripp

Tripp sat around the table, with the rest of the bikers. He was happy to see Mario had joined them. Dagger was still pouting in the corner, but the brothers just ignored him.

"It's time to figure out how to take this fucker down," Preacher ordered. "The injury he gave Fable could have been life threatening."

"Anybody got anything on why Gabe wants her?" Steele questioned.

"It's not sexual or an infatuation," Tripp told the brothers. "I actually think he doesn't like her."

"I may have found something," Mario said. "I don't want to say anything this early, because it's just a hunch, based on a small piece of information I found," he explained. "But I should know for sure in the next day or two."

"Okay," Preacher responded. "Keep digging and keep us posted. You brothers got Gabe's men out of the hospital okay?" he questioned, as he glanced at the four brothers tasked with that job.

"Piece of cake," Steele chuckled. "The goon in the parking lot was easy, seeing as we could sneak up behind him. Of course, Navaho pretty much took him down on his own. Guy never even saw the brother coming."

"Well the goon in the waiting room saw us," Dagger complained. "There was no way for us to sneak up on him, even Shadow couldn't get to him, and that's saying a lot."

Shadow snorted. "So, your way was better?" he snickered.

"My way worked didn't it," Dagger stated proudly.

"Your way was retarded," Shadow grinned, as he shook his head.

"You gonna explain what Dagger did, or is this a private conversation?" Preacher inquired in annoyance.

"Fucker took one look at the goon sitting in the corner and charged right for him. Literally sprinted across the room and jumped at the guy," Shadow told them. "Fucker was too stunned to even blink, before Dagger's crazy ass slammed into him."

"Jesus Christ," Preacher grumbled. "You guys get worse every day. You bunch are turning into delinquents."

"And you're our ring leader," Dagger smirked.

"Can we get back to Gabe?" Tripp ordered.

Mario leaned forward. "The goons are taken care of, nobody will see them again. Word is, Gabe's shitting bricks. He has no idea what happened to them, and it's got him freaked. We left the car at the hospital so it looks like they just disappeared. The fucker even went to the hospital and asked to see the security tapes. Luckily, I know the head guy there, and I had them before we even left."

"Thank fuck your on our side," Steele smirked. "We're lucky to have you."

"Maybe that's the answer to our problem," Preacher piped up, as he rubbed his chin. "One by one, make Gabe's goons disappear. It will fuck with his head and get rid of his back up at the same time."

Tripp shook his head. "You can't just pick off all those men and not have the cops breathing down your necks. Darren can help out some, but he can't slip all that under the rug," he told the bikers.

"We don't hide them," Dagger grunted.

"So, we shoot them and leave them laying in the street?" Steele questioned. "I think you're really starting to lose it," he told the brother.

Dagger frowned. "What I meant is, we set up a series of accidents. Make it look like the men died from actual mishaps. We don't have to hide the bodies, the cops can't touch us, and it will send Gabe off the deep end," he explained.

"What do you suggest?" Preacher asked.

"Car accidents, gas leaks," Dagger didn't get finished before all the brothers interrupted him.

"No more blowing shit up," they yelled as one.

Chapter 26
Tripp

Tripp eyed the man on the roof from his spot in the bushes. This was ridiculous, but it was the plan the brothers had come up with, and if it messed with Gabe's head it was worth it.

They had done their research since the meeting with Mario two days ago. They now had a file started for each one of his goons, with Fable's help. They didn't tell her why they wanted her to help identify each of Gabe's men, just that they wanted to know who to look out for.

The goon they were watching now was a bit lower on the rung, but it made him perfect for the first victim. The goon had a two-story house, and he was currently up on the peak replacing shingles. He had a ladder placed at the back of the house, and that was their target.

Suddenly from the street out front, they heard Dagger yelling. He was wandering down the middle of the street pretending to be drunk. Tripp and Navaho, who were crouched down in the bushes, chuckled from the brother's antics. He was stumbling and screaming that the marshmallow man from Ghost Busters was chasing him. He was a fantastic actor and was drawing quite a crowd.

The goon on the roof dropped his hammer and moved to the front of the house to watch Dagger's hilarious performance. As soon as he moved to the front peek and was out of sight, both brothers moved. Tripp stayed at the bottom and held the ladder, as Navaho hurried up it.

When Navaho reached the roof, he grabbed the large bag of nails, and slung it over his shoulder. When he had climbed about twelve rungs back down the ladder, he stopped and pulled a small saw out of the inside of his vest. With deft hands, he cut one side of the top six rungs. He then made sure they stayed in place and looked secure, before he hurried back down. The brother was fast, and when he hit the ground both men booted it back to the cover of the bushes.

They heard a siren, and a second later tires screeched as a car stopped beside Dagger. The brothers snickered again, as they heard Darren's voice, yelling at Dagger that he was under arrest for drunk and disorderly conduct. Of course, Dagger fought with him a bit and Darren had to chase him around the neighbourhood. Finally, Darren wrestled him into the car and took off.

Seconds later the goon came back over the peak, and stopped to look around. Not seeing the nails, he immediately started cursing. Then he moved to the ladder and climbed over the side, to make his way down.

As soon as his foot hit the first rung it gave way. The man howled in terror and tried to move his foot to the next rung. Tripp and Navaho watched, as the next rung broke too and the man lost his hold. With arms flailing and a scream to wake the dead, the man fell to the ground.

Both brothers cringed when they heard a sickening crack. The goon was lying there, and his neck was twisted at an unnatural position. Tripp knew without checking that the goon was dead. They backed away from the bushes, grabbed the sabotaged ladder, and hurried to the yard behind his. Jumping the fence, they sprinted around the side of the house, and made their way to the street.

Trike was waiting in a van they had borrowed from Mario. They threw the ladder in the back, then quickly jumped inside as Trike took off.

"Everything good?" Trike asked.

"It's good," Navaho stated calmly.

"Dagger should get an award for his performance though," Shadow snickered. "Fucker puts on a good act."

Trike chuckled. "I would expect nothing less. Brothers fucking funny."

Ten minutes later, they pulled up to the clubhouse. One goon down, seven more to go.

Chapter 27
Fable

Fable was sitting in Misty's cabin, with her and the rest of the girls. Tripp was off doing something he said was club business, and that's all he would tell her. Things were quiet on the Gabe front, and he hadn't tried to come by and see her. But she figured it was only a matter of time before he did.

The girls turned out to be a lot of fun. Cassie and Ali were a blast, and she loved holding baby Catherine. They were currently getting ready for a fire. The guys called, saying they were almost ready, and the girls were anxious to head over to them.

Misty had picked out one of Fable's colourful dresses. It was off the shoulder, short-sleeved, and fell to her knees. It was a baby doll style, which meant it had elastic that drew it in under her breasts, and then it flared out in a short skirt. Her hair was down, with only a tiny braid in the side that she had threaded a thin ribbon through. She had on the same jewellery as before, and just a touch of makeup.

She didn't understand why the girls wanted her so dressed up for the bonfire, but she loved it. Her side was getting better too. The stitches were starting to itch, but it wasn't as painful. Her palm now had a thin ugly looking scar, but it was better than the infected mess it had been before.

The girls left the cabin, and Fable stopped cold at the sight in front of her. A trellis had been set up beside the lake, and someone had covered it in twinkly white lights and spruce tree branches. Bright lanterns hung from the trees, along with pretty white lace dream catchers. All the bikers were present, and she couldn't stop the laugh that bubbled up when she saw they were all barefoot.

"It was Dagger's idea," Sniper chuckled from beside her.

"It fucking wasn't," Dagger yelled, from somewhere in the group, and the bikers all howled.

Tripp stood in the gazebo with Preacher, and he looked handsome in black jeans, his leather cut, and a white dress shirt. They both also wore no shoes.

"What is this?" Fable asked Sniper.

"We're getting married Gypsy. You said yes, so I'm not wasting any more time," Tripp shouted from the gazebo. "Get up here pretty girl and be mine forever."

Tears streamed down her face as she nodded back happily. She went to move forward, but Sniper stopped her.

"We were friends once, a while ago. I know your father died in the mine accident, so I was wondering if you'd let me walk you down the isle," he asked. "Besides, I saved your clothes. You owe me," Sniper smirked.

She smiled at him and placed her hand in his. He instantly pulled her hand to his mouth and kissed the back, before tucking it close to his chest.

"Did you fucking need to kiss her asshole?" Tripp bellowed from the gazebo. "It's my god damned wedding, but I'll still take you down."

Sniper chuckled from beside her and led her down the isle, while Ali played her guitar. As soon as they got close, Tripp snatched her from Sniper and pulled her against him.

The ceremony was perfect, and she loved it. It was even better than the wedding in her dreams. At the end, Tripp gave her a kiss that left her breathless, while the bikers whistled and yelled.

Suddenly she noticed loud sobbing from beside her. Tripp pulled her out of the way as Steele almost ran them over in his haste to get to Cassie.

"What's wrong Little Mouse?" Steele soothed as he pulled her close.

"I'm sorry I wanted to wait a year. I don't want to wait a year anymore. I want you to make me mine too. I just want to be with you," Cassie wailed. Steele was stunned for a minute, then he turned to Fable and Tripp.

"Will it ruin your wedding if we get married too?" he asked.

"No," both of them answered immediately. Then they moved out of the way as Steele and Cassie said their vows as well.

The day was amazing, and Fable couldn't remember being this happy. She was Tripp's now, and nothing would change that.

Chapter 28
Tripp

Tripp's wedding to Fable had been everything he had hoped it to be. His girl was stunning, and she literally glowed as they said their vows. He was fucking thrilled that she was now tied to him forever. No matter what happened from here on out, they would face it together.

He was also happy for his brother Steele. He knew the man wanted nothing more than to officially make Cassie his, but he was trying to give her time. After her first abusive marriage, he understood her trepidation. Now they were together, and the grin he sported showed exactly how much that meant to him.

After the ceremony, the bikers had a huge bonfire. Ali broke out her guitar, and the badasses roasted marshmallows. Dagger, the jackass he was, surprised Raid by handing him a harp. He said he would have gotten it out earlier, but he hadn't wanted to ruin the wedding. True to form, Raid chased him around the yard with it and when he caught him, he broke it over the brothers back. Dagger had pouted as he walked away with a broken piece in each hand.

About two hours into the night, Tripp had enough. He carefully picked up his Gypsy and headed for Trike's cabin. The brother had generously offered him his for the night, seeing as Tripp hadn't started theirs yet. Tripp kicked open the door, then laughed as a shit ton of balloons and streamers assaulted him. They were all a pearly white, and everyone of them said congratulations.

He headed straight for the bedroom and laid his Gypsy on the bed. She immediately grabbed his neck and pulled him down for a kiss. Tripp quickly took over, turning the kiss to a heated one. Even he was breathless, when they finally pulled apart.

Fable watched him curiously as he moved from the bed, and crouched down on the floor. He chuckled when her head popped over the side, trying to see what he was doing. He searched around under the bed and touched the box he was looking for. After a tug, the box was free, and he lifted it onto the bed.

"I wanted to give you this earlier, but I decided it would make a perfect wedding gift. This is just another way to reaffirm that you're mine," Tripp stated, as he pushed the box towards her.

Fable watched him for a minute, then lifted the lid off the box. Her eyes lit up as she saw the leather vest inside and lifted it out. He had the name Gypsy embroidered on a patch on the front, and Property of Tripp was stitched across the back. Tears fell down her cheeks as she stared at the vest lovingly.

"I know it doesn't go with your style," he chuckled. "But I hope you'll wear it anyway."

Fable beamed up at him as she answered. "I love it. It's absolutely perfect, and besides," she grinned, "a biker vest goes with everything."

Tripp smiled at her enthusiasm. "I can't wait to make love to you, with only that vest covering your pretty little body," he smirked.

"I can do that," Fable laughed. "Although I may need some help to get out of these clothes, and into the vest," she whispered seductively.

Tripp pounced then, and she giggled. He was cautious of her side, as he helped her remove the dress and underwear, then he got her into the vest.

"I'll remember the look of you in just this vest for a long time," Tripp admitted. "I love you Gypsy," he told her huskily.

"I love you too Tripp," Fable instantly replied. "Make love to me," she begged. "I want to be yours completely."

"You've always been mine completely," Tripp vowed, then he proceeded to slowly sink into her, and make love to her passionately and carefully. It was a night neither of them would ever forget, and he couldn't be happier. Late into the morning they both fell asleep, and Tripp clung to his Gypsy in happiness. She was back to her old self completely, and Tripp was over the fucking moon.

Chapter 29
Tripp

It had been two days since the wedding, and Tripp had enjoyed every minute together. He had only borrowed Trike's cabin for one night, so unfortunately, they were back in the compound. Lucky for him, his Gypsy didn't seem to care, she loved the way the brothers had done up the room, and she loved the brothers themselves. She called her room their own little oasis.

The brothers all adored her, and she was never without company. They laughed with her, they got her anything she needed, and they treated her like family. There was now a permanent smile on her face. Plus, her and Misty were joined at the hip.

Now that they had discovered each other again, they were never far apart. The other girls were around too, but the two girls seemed to share a special bond that the others didn't have.

Tripp finally decided that regardless of the problems with Gabe, he was starting his cabin. He was done waiting for things to get better, he wanted his girl all to himself. He wasn't necessarily jealous of how Fable got along with the brothers, but they were just around too much.

Fable and him had already discussed the cabin, and they knew where they wanted it. There was a nice grassy lower spot, on a piece of land beside Misty and Trike's cabin. The water was shallower there, and the views were stunning. A lot of the bikers were choosing spots that were just a little bit higher, but Tripp's spot made it seem like the cabin would be in its own little valley.

Preacher immediately gave him the go ahead, and they got to work. Whenever a brother had any free time, they were down at the cabin helping out. Tripp knew it wouldn't be long until the cabin was done. He was hoping it would only take a couple weeks. The brothers were fast, and once they got started, things moved quickly.

Today, Tripp and Dagger were taking a break though. And once again, Tripp found himself hunkered down in a bush. It was time to take out another one of Gabe's goons and keep things moving. Navaho had followed this man for three days, and discovered that each morning he stood beside his car and smoked a cigarette. But the goon didn't have a bucket or anything, that he threw the butt in. He tossed it to the ground and put it out with the heel of his boot.

Dagger of course, had to come along with him for this one. If the job involved any type of explosion, Dagger wanted to be front and centre. Trike had worked on a road crew and had been the brother who knew explosives, but once he taught Dagger, the brother took over, having an instant knack for it. Trike was amazed at how adept the brother had become and willingly handed over the reigns.

Dagger had been the one that had climbed under the car this morning and put a small hole in the gas tank. Slowly but steadily, gas had leaked out, and it now covered the driveway. The brothers were just waiting patiently for the goon to come out.

Twenty minutes later, he stepped out of the house. His cigarette was already lit as he made his way to the car. The brothers had been worried the smell of gas would tip him off, so Dagger had sprayed the area with a flowery room spray. The smell of the spray had dissipated a bit, so now it just smelled like some distant flowers. The idiot was a genius.

Finally, the goon was done his smoke, and he threw it to the driveway. As soon as the end hit the gas, a flame spread along the ground. The goon had only a second to curse, and then the whole car blew, taking him with it. Dagger jumped up and down silently as flames rose high in the sky. The car landed in several pieces, scattered over the driveway, and the goon was gone.

Dagger gave him a high five, then hurried away. Tripp shook his head as he followed the brother back to his bikes. Another one down, only a few more to go.

Chapter 30
Fable

Fable had a feeling things were about to get intense when she was told she would also attend church that day. She was informed by the girls that church was only for the men. They had only gone in one time themselves, and it was extremely important if they wanted her there.

She picked out one of her long skirts and paired it with a short-sleeved blouse. Tripp helped her dress, so it took twice as long as it normally would. The man kept getting distracted, but she loved it, so she didn't complain. The last piece of clothing to go on was her new leather vest. Tripp looked at her proudly when she was done, and she couldn't be happier.

Hand in hand, they made the way to the huge room they would hold the meeting in. It was intimidating to be the last ones to arrive, but the bikers all smiled at her in greeting, easing her nerves. Tripp took a seat and pulled her down on his lap. She didn't complain, loving the possessiveness.

It surprised her to see Mario sitting beside Preacher, but she had no time to ask Tripp about it, as Preacher started the meeting.

"I asked Fable to join us because Mario has finished digging into Gabe, and has found some things that need to be shared," Preacher stated. "I'm not going to say anything else, as I think it's best if Mario explains it himself."

Mario had a huge file in front of him, that he opened and pulled a piece of paper out of. He then slid the paper across the table, so it landed in front of Tripp. Tripp picked it up and held it so they could both see it. Fable was shocked to see it was an article about the mine cave in that killed her father.

"Did you know the families of the miners killed sued the mine for wrongful death and unsafe conditions?" Mario asked her. She stared at him a second, then shook her head no.

"My mom never said anything about it," Fable admitted to him.

"Well it was a group lawsuit, and the families won. It wasn't well publicized, because the mine didn't want it getting out," Mario explained. "Your mother must have wanted nothing to do with the money, because she put it all in a trust fund for you."

Fable shook her head again. "I don't know anything about this," she replied in confusion.

"Maybe your mom wanted to surprise you?" Tripp offered.

"They will release the trust fund to you on your twenty-third birthday," Mario explained.

"But that's in a couple weeks," Fable responded in surprise. "How much is the trust fund worth?" she questioned.

Mario slid another paper across the table to Tripp. When he picked it up, Fable could only stare at the figure.

"Seven hundred and fifty thousand dollars," Fable gasped.

"Yep," Mario acknowledged. "It's the amount of your mothers share of the group settlement."

"So, what does this have to do with Gabe?" Tripp inquired.

"Apparently, when your mother moved to Florida, she signed the house over to you," Mario smirked.

"She did," Fable agreed.

"Well it looks like Gabe snuck some extra papers in with them. He made himself your sole beneficiary. If anything should happen to you, both the trust and the house go directly to him," Mario further explained.

"You've got to be fucking kidding me," Tripp roared. "Are you saying what I think you're fucking saying?" he growled.

Fable could only stare at Tripp in confusion. "What does that mean?" she asked quietly.

"It means I'm gonna string the fucker up by his god damned balls," Tripp roared.

She looked to Mario next, still not understanding.

"It means he plans to either kill you himself, or have someone do it for him, after you turn twenty-three," Mario told her sadly. "Then he'll inherit everything."

"That's why he's so mean to me," Fable said as a tear rolled down her cheek. "He treated me like garbage and isolated me. He probably has my death planned already, and no one would even know I was gone."

"Well I guess we fucked up that plan," Steele snickered. "It's time to step things up on our end," he said. "We have a couple weeks before he can make an attempt on her life. Let's make his life a living hell."

All the brothers roared in agreement, and then Fable settled back against Tripp once more, and listened as the brothers discussed what they would do.

Chapter 31
Tripp

Tripp was furious, hearing all the information about Gabe that Mario had gathered. Fable's own stepbrother was planning to kill her off, just so he could get a hold of her money. He thought about things for a minute, as his detective brain seemed to go into overdrive.

"There must be a reason he needs that money?" Tripp said. "You can't tell me he wants it so he can live here, and work with you in this town," he told Mario.

"I have a theory about that," Mario replied. "He may be using me as a failsafe plan. Have you ever heard the name Tony Ramos?" he asked.

Tripp thought for a minute. "You mean the head of the drug cartel down in Florida. He's on everybody's most wanted list."

"That's the one," Mario agreed. "He has a buy in of a million bucks. Between the trust and the house, he should get that."

"Fuck," Tripp groaned. "That makes perfect sense."

Steele spoke up then. "So, we get the beneficiary changed on the trust and the house, and we make sure this fucker knows you're married now," he said. "We can use the club lawyer. It can be done in the next day or two. Do we have copies of those documents, or does Gabe have them?" Steele questioned.

"I've got copies right here," Mario confirmed, as he held out his folder.

"Okay, so now we just piss him off. I think we should take out another of his goons," Steele pushed. "I want to fuck with him a bit."

"Does he have any regular haunts, maybe somewhere he eats or drinks regularly? I need it to be a public place," Preacher questioned.

"He has lunch on the patio at the bistro every Thursday," Fable told them. "He leaves around noon," she added.

"Okay," Mario grinned. "Tomorrow I'll have a meeting with him. I'll explain he's an ass, and not someone I want to do business with. You guys take out another goon, and on Thursday, we make a show of eating at the same restaurant as him. I want him to see me with you after I've kicked him to the curb. He needs to see that Fable is married, and I think he needs to see the club vest on her too."

"I think that's a fucking great idea," Tripp snickered. "Do we have a good hacker in the group?" he asked.

"My man Trent works miracles," Mario told them.

"Tell him to get in touch with me. I have an idea I want to run by him," Tripp ordered.

"Will do," Mario answered.

"Okay," Preacher piped up. "Meeting adjourned. We have a goon to kill, a lawyer to get in touch with, and a lunch to make reservations for."

All the bikers chuckled as they rose and headed out of the room. Fable watched them, not sure how to feel about everything that had been revealed.

"I want this over," she told Tripp sadly. "And I don't want to die."

Tripp pulled her closer. "Honey, once he finds out we're married and his name is off the paperwork, he won't have a leg to stand on. I have a couple other ideas I want to start on as well. I want to drive the fucker nuts," Tripp growled.

"Okay, let's do this," Fable agreed. Then she held up her hand for a high five. Tripp stared at her hand with a smirk on his face.

"You want to high five," he chuckled.

"I want to start out with a high five," Fable told him. "Then we can move this to the bedroom."

"Best fucking wife ever," Tripp grinned. Then he gave her a high five, picked her up, and stomped out of the room, heading down the hall. She ignored the catcalls and whistles that followed them. But Tripp apparently didn't.

"We're fucking newlywed's assholes," Tripp shouted. Then he made love carefully to he, for the rest of the afternoon. She was almost asleep, when he kissed her deep and told her goodbye. Apparently, he was off to kill a goon.

Chapter 32
Tripp

The next goon the brothers decided to take out, was the one Gabe relied on the most. He kept Gabe's finances, and he gave the fucker a lot of advice. Without him, Gabe would be lost. It was perfect. They wanted to bring on the heat, and this was the best way to do it.

They did a lot of research on the man and didn't find much. But then Trent had a breakthrough. The goon had been admitted to the hospital two times, and both times it had been for a bee sting. Apparently, the guy was incredibly allergic to bees, to the point it was life threatening.

That was their in. They knew of several abandoned farms just down the road from the compound. Of course, they put Navaho in charge of this task, seeing as he was their best bet. And of course, Dagger was told to stay at the compound. One wrong move from the fucker, and they'd all be in trouble.

The mission was simple, search the farms, and come back with a large wasp nest. They hoped to find one either growing on the side of the houses, or attached to the crumbling barns. Tripp went too, a little warily, along with Sniper and Raid. The rest of the brothers opted out of this one.

They were successful at the second farm. The house was a rundown one story, and there was a huge nest growing in the porch's corner. Navaho held a large flat ended shovel, and Raid held a large burlap bag. Both brothers wore large thick gloves, and long sleeves. They approached slowly as Tripp and Sniper watched from the yard.

Raid stopped directly under the nest and held the bag open. Navaho raised the shovel and moved it towards the top of the nest. There were a few wasps flying close by, but they didn't give the brothers any trouble.

Suddenly, Navaho struck. He shoved the end of the shovel flat against the roof and literally cut the nest down. It dropped into the bag Raid held out. Raid quickly pulled the drawstrings tight, shutting the bees inside. Then the brothers booted it, jumping off the porch and pounding across the yard. They weren't taking any chances with the few bees that were left buzzing around the porch.

As soon as they got close, Sniper held out a large Tupperware container, and Raid dropped the bag inside. They snapped the lid on, and the men headed back to the truck they had arrived in. It only took a minute to lift the container into the back.

They drove directly to the goon's house and parked just down from it. They took the container out, and hurried through the trees and around to his backyard. The goon was leaning against the side of the house, watching as his dog chased a ball.

Navaho nodded to Sniper, and the brother cautiously opened the container. Luckily, the drawstring held and the bees were still inside the bag. The brothers watched in awe, as Navaho pulled a pipe out of his vest pocket, lit it, and began to smoke. No one had any idea what he was doing, but nobody said a word.

After a minute, Navaho approached the bag, opened it a tiny bit, and blew the smoke inside. The bees that were buzzing around a minute before instantly calmed down. He did this three more times, then dropped the sides of the bag to the ground. There were a few bees flying around, but they appeared sleepy.

Before the brothers could blink, Sniper picked up the huge nest, and threw it as hard as he could at the side of the house. It hit about a foot from the goon's head and broke open. The goon jumped, then started screaming and flailing his arms about, as the bees attacked. He tried to run, but he only made it a couple steps before falling to the ground.

The brothers watched, as the goons body jerked every time they stung him. Slowly, the jerking got less and less, until finally he didn't jerk at all. Since Dagger wasn't with them, there was no cheering or fanfare. The brothers picked up the empty bag and container, and headed back to the truck as silently as they had arrived. And surprisingly, not one of them ended up stung.

Chapter 33
Tripp

The next afternoon, Fable and Tripp met with the club's lawyer. It only took a few minutes to sign the paperwork she had prepared for them. Fable couldn't be happier, now that Tripp was her sole beneficiary. Gabe had been taken off the document.

Mario had left the folder with everything he had dug up and all the paperwork with Tripp. Fable sat quietly for a minute as she flipped through it, searching for something.

"What are you up to Gypsy?" Tripp asked, after the lawyer had left. They were sitting in the common room and were surrounded by most of the brothers. As church was supposed to be for just the men and they were only signing papers, they had opted to stay out here.

"I want a meeting with Darren, and a real estate agent as soon as possible," Fable replied quietly.

Without even asking why, Tripp called Darren and asked him to come by the clubhouse right away. Preacher also called a realtor he knew and arranged for her to come by right away too.

Twenty minutes later, both were sitting at a table with them, and all the bikers had moved in closer. Fable pulled out the deed to the house, and passed it to Tara, the real estate agent.

"I want to sell my house," Fable explained to Tara. "And I want it done immediately."

Tripp instantly turned to her. "But that's your house," he stated.

"I know," Fable whispered. "But we're married now, I want my cabin."

Tripp smiled at her as he leaned over and kissed her deeply. "I'll gather the brothers, and get it finished," he declared. "Okay?"

"Okay," Fable repeated back.

The real estate agent smiled at them. "I'm good at my job," she grinned. "If you don't mind getting a bit less than what it's worth, I can sell it within a couple days."

"That sounds perfect," Fable told her. Tara pulled out a form and passed it to her, along with a pen.

"This is just a declaration stating I have the authority to act and make decisions on your behalf with regard to the property. This way I don't have to stop and get in touch with you every time something comes up. I can handle all the details, and keep moving things along," Tara explained.

Fable signed the paper and passed it back to her. The agent put it in her briefcase and then turned back to her.

"Is the house occupied, or is it vacant?" Tara questioned. Fable turned to Darren then.

"That's why I need you," Fable replied. "Gabe still lives there, but the property's in my name. How can

I get him out?" The bikers all started snickering as they realized what she was doing.

"If the house is solely in your name, you can basically kick him out whenever you want. He has no leg to stand on," Darren said.

"Right, and do I have to tell him in person?" Fable asked.

"Legally, it's your safest move. But you need witnesses, I should probably be there," Darren smiled happily. "And I was worried that things were settling down with Tripp off the force."

Tripp gave him the finger. "We have the lunch planned for today, how about we do this first thing tomorrow morning? Can you be at her house for around nine?" Tripp inquired.

Darren smirked. "Wouldn't miss it," he promised. The real estate agent smiled then as well.

"I can do a drive by, and check to see what other houses in the area have sold for. I'll drop the price by at least ten thousand. Do you want me there with the for-sale sign at nine?" Tara asked.

"That would be wonderful," Fable agreed. "I'm sure a couple of the guys will come with me, so they can make sure you're safe."

"Ah Darling," Preacher said. "Half the club will be there."

"Okay," Fable blinked, as she looked back at Tara. "I'll be surprised if Gabe will even be able to see us behind the wall of badass muscle," she admitted. The bikers all chuckled as they moved away.

"I'll bring the dynamite," Dagger yelled from the far end of the room.

"No dynamite," they all yelled back at him.

Chapter 34
Fable

Fable was surrounded as they walked into the bistro. Mario had made arrangements for them to have a large table outside on the patio, extremely close to Gabe's. The hostess paled when she looked up and found them all standing in front of her.

"Reservation for Mario," Mario requested politely.

She stared at him for a minute, blinked, and grabbed a ton of menus. Then without a word, turned and led the way to the patio. Fable looked around at all the bikers and giggled, Gabe would definitely freak. Her, Tripp and Mario were there, along with Preacher, Steele, Dragon, Dagger and Navaho.

The waitress turned and pointed to the table that had been prepared for them. "The other member of your party has already arrived," she let them know.

Fable could only look at Tripp in question. But, when they reached the table, he burst out laughing.

"Couldn't resist could you buddy," Tripp snickered.

"Hell no," Darren replied, as he grinned back at his old partner. "Now have a seat before the little prick arrives."

The bikers shook their heads, but did as advised. Beers were flowing, and the men were laughing, when Gabe and two of his men were escorted to his table. He stopped and stared at them for a minute, then glared as he sat in his usual spot.

The men chuckled when Mario waved at him, and he turned a dark shade of red. "I told him to fuck off," Mario told them all. "He didn't take it very well."

"Shots all around," Dagger shouted to the waitress. "We're celebrating a marriage today." She hurried away to get them and returned a moment later with a large tray. Even Fable had a shot. Dagger stood, and cleared his throat, as the bikers smirked at him.

"I'd like to propose a toast," Dagger stated. "To the prettiest little bohemian chick I know, and the craziest ex cop in the group."

"I'm the only ex cop in the group," Tripp chuckled.

"Yeah," Darren declared with a shake of his head. "I can't quit, because you need me to cover up all your shit up."

Dagger stared at him hard, trying to intimidate Darren, but the cop just laughed and waved him on.

"To Tripp and Fable, may your life be filled with mayhem and mischief," Dagger roared.

The brothers cheered, and then a chair hitting the ground had them turning.

"What the fuck?" Gabe roared. "You married that asshole," he yelled at her. Fable moved closer to Tripp and stood slightly in front of him.

"I most certainly did. And if you hadn't gotten involved, we would have done this a lot sooner," Fable sneered angrily.

"What the fuck are you wearing anyway? You look like a whore," Gabe snarled. "And is that a god damned biker vest?"

Fable had worn one of her short, off the shoulder baby doll dresses. Her hair was down, and she had a scarf wrapped in it. She wore sparkly sandals and had finished the outfit off with her new leather vest. At Gabe's words, all the bikers pushed their chairs back, and stood.

"What the fuck did you just call my wife?" Tripp roared. Fable watched as Gabe turned a horrible white colour.

"Waitress," Gabe yelled. "I need my cheque."

"You're gonna need a hospital too," Tripp snarled.

That's when the waitress came out with his cheque. She hurried to ring through his card, then looked at him in confusion.

"I'm sorry sir," she stammered. "I'm afraid your card has been reported as stollen. It's advising me to call the police."

Darren immediately moved forward. "Sir, I'm placing you under arrest for theft," he informed Gabe.

Gabe just sputtered. "But it's my credit card. How the hell can I steal my own credit card?"

"Turn around and place your hands behind your back," Darren ordered. Gabe finally did, and as Darren led him out, Gabe was still shouting.

"It's my god damned credit card."

"This fucking with Gabe plan sure is fun," Dagger laughed. "I can't wait until tomorrow when we put the house up for sale."

Chapter 35
Tripp

It was about a half hour before they were to be at Fable's, and they were just about ready to go. Fable was dressed in the jeans he had bought her, along with a pretty black t-shirt with a dream catcher pattern on the front. She had short black fringed boots on her feet, and her vest on. They were currently arguing.

"Gypsy," Tripp pleaded. "You still need help to get dressed, you're not healed enough to ride on the back of my bike. Cassie offered her truck, I think we should just go in that."

He growled when she picked up one of her colourful pillows and threw it at him. Obviously, she didn't agree with him.

"We sleep cuddling and I wrap my arms around you, how is that different?" Fable argued.

He sighed. "The vibration may hurt you, and I can't stand to see you in pain."

"I can handle it," Fable pushed, as she placed her hands on her hips. "It's been a lifetime since I've been on the back of your bike. I miss it," she said sadly. Tripp missed it too, and he was dying to agree, but he was still worried.

"I don't know," Tripp sighed.

"Listen," Fable pleaded. "It's only a fifteen-minute ride. Maybe Cassie could drive the truck, and if it hurts, I'll let you know. You can pull over and I can get off."

He smirked at her. "You wouldn't tell me if you were hurting, even if you were dying."

She tilted her head and said quietly. "We just got married. I'm feeling better, and I want to ride on the back of my badass husband's bike."

Tripp growled again as he stalked towards her. When he was close, he grabbed the braid she had put her hair in and tilted her head back. Then he slammed his mouth against hers, kissing her thoroughly and for a long time. Finally, after what felt like forever, he pulled back.

"Gypsy, you don't play fair," Tripp rasped. "And if we didn't have to leave now, I'd take you back to bed, and show you how much those words mean to me," he told her. She shivered, as she placed her tiny hands on his chest.

"Is that a yes?" Fable questioned hopefully.

"It's a hell yes," Tripp chuckled. Then he took her hand and led her out to the common room. It surprised them to see it was completely empty.

"Where is everybody?" Fable questioned.

"I have absolutely no idea," Tripp admitted. He headed towards the door and pushed it open.

When they stepped outside, it was to see the entire club already on their Harley's and waiting for them. When Tripp looked down at his Gypsy, he saw tears in her eyes.

"What the fuck are you staring at?" Preacher yelled. "We've been sitting out here forever. Get on your god damned motorcycle and let's go," he ordered.

Tripp smirked at his prez, then led Fable to his Harley. He strapped a helmet on her head, then climbed on. He kicked up the kickstand, placed his feet on the ground, and steadied the bike. Fable grinned as she placed her hands on his shoulders, put her foot on the peg, and lifted her other leg over the seat. When she was settled, she wrapped her arms around his waist.

Tripp couldn't resist twisting his neck and stealing another kiss. She immediately complied.

"Oh, come on," Dagger yelled. "We've got the head goon to piss off. Can we wait until later to do that shit?"

Tripp ended the kiss and faced forward once more. Instead of answering, he fired up his Harley and revved the engine. Preacher gave the signal, and all the other bikes roared to life. The sound was defeating, and the ground shook. Tripp loved it. He squeezed Fables leg, then followed the bikes out. He was right in the middle of the group. The brothers always placed a member who had a woman on his bike in that position. It was a protective measure.

Tripp couldn't be happier. Fable was now his wife, she was on the back of his bike again, and she was back to herself. Now all they needed to do was get rid of Gabe, then everything would be perfect.

Chapter 36
Fable

As soon as they pulled up in front of her house, Gabe was on the front lawn glaring at them all. She didn't doubt for a minute, that the loud roar from all the Harley's drew his attention long before they came into sight. Both the real estate agent and Darren were parked a couple houses back, so they walked up to meet them.

"What the fuck do you all want?" Gabe yelled, as he moved down the front steps. He stopped when he reached the bottom and didn't go any further. Suddenly, his eyes narrowed as he got a good look at Fable.

"Yesterday, when I saw that god damned dress you were wearing, I had questions, but I thought maybe I was mistaken. Today, seeing you in those butt ugly jeans, I know I'm right. I burned those fucking things, how the hell did you get them back?" Gabe questioned.

Sniper snickered from beside her and Tripp, catching Gabe's attention. "That would be me and my sister," he admitted. "We lived beside you and Fable for about a year." Gabe studied him a minute, then it appeared a light bulb went off.

"The soldier and the blind bitch," Gabe sneered, as he snapped his fingers. Trike immediately turned menacing. He stalked up the front walk and punched Gabe right in the mouth. The man dropped like a sack of potatoes. He wasn't unconscious, but it was obvious he was hurting.

"You ever call my wife that again, I'll break your jaw so bad you'll never talk again," Trike vowed. Then he turned and made his way back to the sidewalk, to stand beside Sniper.

"I was going to do that," Sniper complained.

"Yeah, well she's my wife, so I trump you," Trike explained.

"How the fuck does that trump me, she's my sister?" Sniper argued.

"Yep, but she sleeps in my bed every night," Trike smirked. Sniper instantly put his hands over his ears.

"I don't want to hear that," Sniper snarled.

"What does you living beside me have to do with her clothes?" Gabe questioned, distracting the men.

"Oh, I snuck over and rescued her clothes," Sniper admitted.

"I watched them fucking burn," Gabe argued.

"No, you watched my old clothes, and some old bedding burn," Sniper told an angry Gabe.

"Fucking hell," Gabe huffed. Then he turned his attention back to Fable. "Why the fuck are you here?" he growled.

Fable smiled, as she looked at him. "This is still my house, and I don't want you here anymore. I'm here to kick you out, effective immediately," she happily told him.

"I'm your brother," Gabe roared. "You can't kick me out, it's my house too."

"Actually, she can," Tripp replied. "Her name is the only name on the deed, and you're not a blood relative." Gabe smiled then, and Fable knew it was a sinister one.

"I'm her beneficiary, so my names on it," Gabe sneered.

"Ah, no it's not," Fable told him. "I never signed anything giving you that right."

"Not knowingly," Gabe smiled cruelly. "But I guarantee you did."

"Fine," Fable consented. "But I married Tripp, which automatically makes him my beneficiary. And if that isn't enough, we updated the paperwork. Your name isn't on anything now."

Gabe looked ready to blow. "Well I'm not leaving," he said, as he placed his hands on his hips and stared at them.

That's when Darren got to step in. "Well, that's why I'm here. I'd be more than happy to escort you off the property. I'm sure the men down at the station would love to see you again. What's that, four times this week?" he questioned.

"Four times?" Fable sputtered. But she didn't get to say any more as Gabe lost it.

"Three of my god damned men died this week. One fell off his roof, one blew himself up, and the last one got stung about a hundred times by a swarm of bees. Do you assholes know anything about that?" he roared.

A lot of the bikers chuckled then, only making Gabe madder.

"Sounds to me like the goons suffered a couple nasty accidents," Sniper proclaimed. "You can't pin that on us."

"You've got thirty minutes to get your belongings, and get off the property," Darren explained. "If you don't, I'll have no choice but to arrest you again."

Then Tara promptly walked up with the for-sale sign and shoved it into the ground.

Chapter 37
Tripp

Tripp couldn't be happier when Gabe went back inside the house to gather his shit. It looked like the goon was actually gonna make this easier. The brothers settled in, knowing Gabe would probably take the full thirty minutes Darren had given him. When he glanced down at Fable, she seemed relieved as well.

Slowly, boxes piled up in the driveway at the side of the house. Gabe was quiet and efficient as he gathered his things. After fifteen minutes, Darren caught Gabe, as he came out with another box.

"Fifteen minutes left. Just grab the essentials, the boys can drop off the stuff you leave behind somewhere for you," Darren told him. Gabe just nodded and headed back inside.

Suddenly, Tara appeared beside them.

"Can you show me around? I want to see what I have to work with," she asked Fable.

Fable shrugged. "Sure, I guess, it won't take too long, right?"

"Nope," Tara answered. "A quick peek, then I can be out of your hair."

Tripp immediately halted the rest of their conversation. "That fucker has fifteen more minutes, Darren just gave him the warning. Even with me and the boys with you, I don't want you in the house with him. You can certainly look around the outside, but that's it. Once he's gone, you've got free rein, but for now, please do as I ask," he requested.

Fable nodded at him, then stood on her tippy toes to kiss his chin. Tripp laughed at their height difference, then grabbed her around the waist, and picked her up. He kissed her the way he wanted to.

It was long, it was deep, and it always left her slightly dazed looking. He only stopped because the whistling got on his nerves. He gave the entire group the finger, then carefully set her down.

"Be good," Tripp ordered. "And stay where we can see you." Then he gave her a pat on the ass and sent her on her way. She turned back to him, and gave him a wink, before leading the agent to the side of the house. He chuckled at her, thrilled that he had her back. Each day he had with her was better than the last.

Sniper and Dragon moved over to him once the girls were gone.

"Married life really suits you," Dragon grinned. "It's nice to see you finally relaxing and enjoying life."

Tripp dropped his head. "Yeah, I guess I was just never cut out to be a cop. This is where I was meant to be, I just wish I figured that out sooner," he admitted.

"Nah," Sniper replied. "I think you wanted it in the beginning. But loosing your girl shifted your priorities. You were in a bad place for a long time, and you lost interest in it."

"I agree," Dragon nodded. "Now you have your girl, the stress of the job's gone, and you can ride your Harley during the day instead of sneaking around in the dark."

"Fuck me," Tripp huffed. "Does everyone know I used to ride it at night?" All the brothers within hearing distance nodded yes.

"For a detective, you don't have the stealthy stuff down very good," Navaho snickered, from where he leaned against his bike. "I used to follow you sometimes. Did you know that?" he asked.

Tripp stared at the brother dumb founded. "No fucking way." he protested.

"Yep, you used to ride past her house every Saturday night. Then, you'd go park down by the lake, and stare at the water for about an hour," Navaho smirked.

"Jesus," Tripp groaned. But he didn't get to say anything else as a bloodcurdling scream came from one of the girls.

The men looked to where they could see the two girls. Tara had been the one to scream. She stumbled towards them unsteadily. Navaho moved quickly, and was the first to reach her. He caught her as she fell. It horrified them to see a knife sticking out of her back.

Tripp headed for Fable, but he was too late. Gabe had grabbed her around the waist and held another knife to her neck, as he dragged her into the house. Blood was already trickling down from a small cut.

"You come anywhere near this house, I'll kill her," Gabe ordered. Then he disappeared inside, and Tripp heard the click of the lock behind him.

Chapter 38
Fable

Fable was happy to show the real estate agent the house. She was looking forward to selling it and making a new home with Tripp. When her father had died in the mining accident, the house had changed for her. Without her father around, it wasn't home. She missed his presence, she missed his laughter, and she missed his love.

The real estate agent was asking her questions, but she was half listening. Honestly, she was watching Tripp. He was talking and laughing with his club brothers, and she loved it. He had changed a lot since they had been together. Before he had been carefree and loving, and he had big dreams. Now he seemed more intense, angrier, and his love was fiercer somehow too. His protectiveness was through the roof, and she loved that. She could definitely admit, she loved the twenty-five year old version of him better.

She turned to the real estate agent, meaning to ask her to repeat herself, when the side door was thrown open. Tara had her back to the door and never saw the knife that Gabe plunged into her back. Fable could only watch in horror as Tara screamed and stumbled away. Fable tried to run, but Gabe was there in an instant. He grabbed her around the waist, slammed her back against his chest, and shoved a knife against her throat.

When she looked up, Tripp and the bikers were running towards them, but she knew they wouldn't make it. Gabe was already backing towards the door. She watched as Navaho reached the agent first, just as she fell. He was quick and caught her before she hit the ground. Fable could only hope the poor girl was okay.

Fable caught Tripp's eyes, just before Gabe dragged her into the house. His showed pure devastation, and she hated that, but they also showed a fierce determination. She knew then and there, he'd do anything he had to to get her back.

Gabe shouted something at the men, but she was too focused on Tripp to pay attention, and then they were inside the house, and he was locking the door. As soon as the knife was removed from her throat she fought, but Gabe was a lot bigger than her, and one quick blow to the head caused her to see stars.

She was helpless and slightly dizzy, as Gabe dragged her through every room on the bottom floor, closing curtains, and moving furniture he had placed beside the doors in front of them. She realized that he had used his half hour to plan this, and not to pack his things.

He pulled her up the stairs and threw her on the floor of his room. She had no time to react, as he pinned her down, and held her arm against the floor. With one quick move, he shoved the knife he had been holding right through the centre of her hand. She screamed in pain, as fire spread through her hand, it felt like he had cut if off.

Next, he twisted, and reached for another knife on the nightstand. Then he drove that one into the fleshy part of her opposite shoulder, driving it right through and into the floor. Black spots danced before her eyes and she almost blacked out, as she tried not to throw up from the agony she felt. Gabe had effectively secured her to the floor. She couldn't move either arm, to remove the knives.

"Aww," Gabe snarled. "You look so pretty like that. I'd love to see you get out of that one." He turned as he heard some loud banging from outside. She knew all the men had heard her scream, it was just a matter of holding on now until they could get to her.

"You stay here," Gabe laughed. "I'll be back in a minute." Then she watched as he hurried from the room.

She tried to move the arm that had the knife in her shoulder, but even the tiniest movement pulled at the knife and cut her more. The only thing left to do, was scream as loud as she could, to let the men know where in the house she was. So that's what she did.

Chapter 39
Tripp

Tripp couldn't reach Fable before the door was closed, and Gabe flipped the lock. It was a steel door, and he knew it would take a while to get through it. He roared in agony, knowing they had pushed Gabe too far. With no leverage now to keep her alive until her birthday, Gabe would most likely kill her.

Tripp pounded on the door, then tried to kick it right beside the handle, to break the lock. The door cracked from the force of his boot, but didn't break. He raised his foot again, getting ready to kick, when Sniper grabbed him and pulled him back.

"Stop," Sniper roared. "And calm the fuck down. I need about thirty seconds to organize this, then we go in."

Tripp stopped and eyed his brother fearfully. "I need in there now," he cried.

"We know," Raid sighed sympathetically. "But Sniper, Shadow and me have been in situations like this before, although this time we don't have insurgents firing at us from outside as well."

Sniper turned to Shadow. "What's our best bet?" he asked, as all the men gathered around to hear what Shadow had to say.

Just as Shadow went to talk, a blood-curdling scream came from the top floor. Tripp went to run back towards the house, but Steele and Dragon grabbed him, effectively stopping him. Shadow made sure he was secure, then he turned back to face everyone.

"I want men at every window and door. When I say go, we're gonna hit every fucking way in at once. Use patio furniture, use your spare helmets, whatever it takes to break through. I also want men hitting the upstairs windows. Throw things at them to break them, I don't care what you use," Shadow ordered.

Another scream rent the air, and the men tensed. Fable was alive, but it was obvious he was hurting her. Tripp couldn't stand it.

"Where'd the scream come from?" Sniper asked him.

"I think it's the back bedroom, but I can't be positive," Tripp admitted.

"If we don't know for sure, he'll kill her before we get to her," Sniper growled.

Just then another scream came, but this one went on for a while. Tripp listened closely, and knew for sure that it was the back bedroom.

"Back bedroom," he confirmed. "Two windows, one on each side, plus a second window on the north side, that leads into an attached bath."

"Right," Shadow nodded. "I saw a drain pipe, myself Sniper and Raid can climb up and break through the three windows at once. Tripp, I want you banging on the door. Keep at it and don't fucking stop. It will distract him. Brothers go get your things. Navaho, in two minutes exactly you whistle and everyone goes in. Lock and load, but be careful brothers, I don't want Fable hit."

Navaho nodded, and set his watch, then all the brothers moved out. Tripp stood silently as the three scary ass military men took off for the back of the house, then he moved back towards the door. He pounded, he kicked, and he roared, doing everything he could to distract the fucker inside.

His heart almost stopped, when the screaming got quieter and quieter, and finally stopped altogether. He watched as his brothers came back with chairs, tire irons, and some just holding the ends of their guns. They stood at all the windows and doors and waited for Navaho's whistle.

It surprised Tripp when Darren came up beside him carrying a ram. All the detectives had one in the trunk of their cars. They constantly had to get into locked houses, and with this tool, they could hit the door and bust the lock. Darren held one side, and Tripp nodded his thanks, as he grabbed the other.

Seconds later, Navaho whistled, and all hell broke loose. Tripp just prayed they weren't too late.

Chapter 40
Fable

Fable screamed as long as she could before giving up. She just didn't have the energy anymore, and she was sure the bikers would know where she was by now. Her shoulder was still throbbing, and the pain was intense, but her hand didn't hurt as much. That either meant it wasn't as bad as it looked, or it was a lot worse.

Fable was getting cold, but knew it was probably from the blood loss. She could feel the wetness underneath her and knew it was the blood pooling below her. She could still hear the pounding from downstairs, but it was getting quieter now. She really wanted to close her eyes, but knew that was a bad idea.

Eventually Fable heard Gabe's footsteps on the stairs, and knew he was returning. It was obvious, from the look on his face, that he was panicking now.

"You planned out how to grab me, but you didn't plan out how to get out of this," she whispered. His eyes had an almost faraway look to them, and she knew he was losing it.

"No, I fucking didn't. I just wanted to make you and the bikers pay. You ruined my life you know?" Gabe sneered. "I had plans to move back to Florida and buy into a crime bosses empire. I could have made a shit ton of dough," he told her.

"I hated you when I saw you," Gabe went on. "You were like a god damned flower child. You dressed like one, you acted like one, and your fucking mother encouraged it. Then I found the paperwork and got to thinking. The best thing I did, was convince my father to move back and take her with him. Once they were gone, I could get the ball moving." He paused then as he paced the room.

"You were engaged to a god damned cop, and I couldn't have that. Once I got rid of him and all your friends, it was easy. You listened to me then and did what you were told. But you passed him on the fucking street, and that was the beginning of the end. I figured maybe I could work with Mario for a while. But he strung me along and then kicked me to the curb. How was I supposed to know he was on good terms with the fucking bikers? Then the asshole cop joined them." He threw his hands up in the air then.

"And you god damned married him," Gabe roared. Then he stopped as a loud whistle sounded from somewhere outside.

All at once, banging and glass breaking sounded from everywhere in the house, even the upstairs. Gabe flipped out. He headed for the hall, and actually got to the top of the stairs before running back into the room.

He grabbed two more knives off the nightstand, then headed towards her. He barely got one positioned against her throat when the two windows in the room were broken. She could only watch as Sniper and Raid came flying through them. The men aimed their guns at Gabe, but didn't move.

Suddenly, Tripp came barreling through the door, and the sight of her stopped him cold. There was more pounding on the stairs, then the doorway was full of bikers. Gabe kneeled beside her, and at the angle she was at, she could just see them all. But she could also see the bathroom, and knew Gabe couldn't. So, he had no idea that a furious looking Shadow stood in the doorway.

"Don't any of you come any fucking closer," Gabe roared hysterically. "I warned you I'd kill her, and I fucking meant it," he yelled. "I know I'm gonna die, but you bet your fucking ass, she'll go first."

The bikers and Tripp didn't move a muscle, but she watched in fascination, as Shadow crept towards them. The biker was so quiet, he didn't make a sound.

Gabe though was done talking, and she screamed, when he put pressure on the knife at her throat.

Chapter 41
Tripp

The sight of Fable horrified Tripp. Gabe had practically staked his Gypsy to the fucking floor. He could feel his brothers behind him, and he knew Sniper and Raid stood in the corner of the room, but he refused to take his eyes off the knife that was placed against her delicate throat. There was only a small drop of blood, so he knew Gabe wasn't putting much pressure on it yet.

Tripp knew Shadow was approaching, but he refused to look up, and unintentionally let Gabe know the brother was there. The fucker was spewing crap about knowing he was gonna die and taking out Fable first.

As soon as Gabe pushed down on the knife, Shadow lunged. The brother was incredibly fast, as he dove and hit upwards, just beside Fable's head. The brother's fist hit the knife handle dead centre, and startled Gabe, causing him to let it go. Tripp watched, as the knife flew through the air and imbedded itself in the far wall.

Then Gabe was on the ground, with Shadow's knee in his neck. The fucker struggled for a minute, then went limp. And that's when Tripp was able to move. In seconds he was across the room and brushing his Gypsy's hair out of her face. He was happy to see that the cut at her neck was no deeper. Shadow had just proved to him how good he was at his former job.

"Get Doc up here fucking now," Tripp roared, as he stared at his wife. "Hang in there Gypsy, we'll get you out of here in a minute," he tried to sooth. But his girl just smiled up at him.

"I'm okay," Fable whispered. "I can't feel my hand," she admitted.

Tripp had tears in his eyes as he looked at her bludgeoned hand. "I swear to god he'll pay for this," he promised. Then out of the corner of his eye, he saw Navaho and Trike drag a still unconscious Gabe out of room.

Shadow moved back beside him, and knelt as well, placing his hand on Tripp's shoulder. "You're gonna have to keep your cool brother, we need to pull these knives out in a minute, and you're gonna have to help her stay calm."

Tripp nodded his understanding and watched as Raid threw a pile of towels by Fable's head. Finally, the brothers in the room moved to the side, as Doc came barreling up the stairs. He took one look at Fable and cringed, then he barked orders.

"It looks like she's lost a lot of blood, we have to get the knives out now. Tripp stay at her head and keep her calm. Hold both sides of her face and make sure she keeps her eyes on you. It's okay if she passes out, that will happen anyway," Doc explained.

"Shadow, I want you at the knife in her hand, and Sniper, I need you at the knife in her shoulder. When I say go, you pull straight up, as quickly as you can. Raid kneel by Sniper, and when he gets that knife out, you get in there and hold the towels on either side of the wound. I'll do the same to her hand," Doc told them.

Once everyone was in place, they were ready to go. Tripp watched as tears flowed from Fable's eyes. "Thank you," she whispered to everyone in the room.

"Your family honey," Shadow told her, then Doc yelled go.

Both Shadow and Sniper pulled fast, and Fable screamed. They jumped out of the way as Doc and Raid covered the wounds in towels, and applied pressure. Thankfully, that's when his Gypsy passed out.

"She'll be okay," Doc assured him. "The knife in her shoulder went right through, so that's good. The knife in her hand knocked a couple bones. I won't know how bad it is until we get her to the hospital, but she'll be okay," he said.

Tripp nodded, then he picked her up and hurried down the stairs, with Raid and Doc following, holding the towels in place. Tripp would go to the hospital and make sure she was okay, then he'd be dealing with Gabe. And he could guarantee, it would be fucking messy.

Chapter 42
Tripp

Tripp held onto Fable the entire way to the hospital. He was squished into the backseat of Darren's car, with Raid and Doc on either side of him. They still had a tight hold on the towels to stop the blood flow. Unfortunately, the towels were soaked through, and so was her shirt.

They had completely destroyed her vest, and he knew it would upset her. The knife had gone right through it, and Raid was having a hard time holding the towels against her shoulder with it there. So, Sniper had no choice but to pull his switchblade and cut it off her. Preacher had watched him do it, and had nodded his consent, so Tripp knew another vest would be made right away.

Preacher, being the president, was in charge of who got the vests and when. He was also the man that provided them. All Tripp had to do was tell Preacher he wanted one for his girl, and the prez had placed the order. Apparently, he had an older woman that made the vests by hand in her home. Steele and Dragon were the only two other brothers who knew who the lady was.

Gypsy moved in his arms, so he looked down, and was surprised to see her eyes were open.

"Where are we?" she asked weakly.

"In Darren's car and on the way to the hospital," Tripp told her.

"The real estate agent?" she asked.

"An ambulance took her away," Doc answered for him. "Tara was awake and talking when she left, so it looks like she'll be okay." Fable nodded her thanks.

Finally, Darren arrived. He pulled up to the emergency entrance, flashed his badge, then opened the door for them. It was an awkward shuffle thing they had to do to get out, and then they were hurrying through the doors.

"This is becoming a regular thing," the security guard yelled as they passed him. "You need your own entrance," he laughed.

"And you need a new job," Doc yelled back. "You'll be gone within the next hour," he vowed, as he led the way to the elevators.

Tripp looked back just before the elevator door closed, to see the guard had paled considerably. The fucker should have just kept his mouth shut.

As soon as Doc reached the operating rooms, he motioned for Tripp to place his Gypsy on one of the gurneys. Immediately Raid and Doc stepped back as two nurses took their place. When they wheeled Fable into the operating room, she yelled at them to stop. With tears in her eyes, she motioned Tripp over.

"I love you Tripp," Fable said. "Promise me everything will be okay, then kiss me," she ordered. Tripp immediately complied.

"Everything will be okay Gypsy," he easily promised. "Besides, we have some kids to make," he said with a smirk. Her face instantly relaxed, and she smiled at him.

"I want them right away," she insisted.

"Then we'll have to get to work as soon as Doc lets you out of here," Tripp agreed. He leaned down and gave her another long, deep kiss. "I'll be right here waiting for you," he promised, before they whisked away her with Doc hurrying after them.

They all headed down the hall to wash the blood off their hands, then headed to the waiting room. Minutes later, the entire room was full of bikers. Preacher was the first to approach him.

"I left Snake, Navaho and Dagger behind to clean up the mess. They'll fix all the windows and doors and get the blood off the floor. Darren can cover up some things, but we need it done before someone asks too many questions. I also checked in at the nurse's station. Tara's still in surgery, but they'll keep us informed of her condition," Preacher explained.

"Right," Tripp replied in thanks. "When she gets out, I want to kill Gabe, then I want the cabin finished."

"Sounds good," Preacher agreed. "Although once the brothers find out she's okay, they'll probably head back to work on the cabin anyway. That's what they did with the other girls."

Tripp smiled as he looked around the waiting room. Joining The Stone Knight's was the best thing he'd ever done.

Chapter 43
Fable

When Fable woke, she knew she was in Tripp's arms. His smell was surrounding her, and she immediately snuggled back against him. He chuckled and then pulled her even closer.

"You're awake," he whispered in her ear. She shivered slightly, then tilted her head back to look at him. He looked extremely tired, but extremely handsome.

"I am," she agreed. "Can I go home now?" Fable whispered. He chucked again.

"You just got out of surgery," Tripp told her.

"Will I live?" she asked. When he nodded, she smiled. "Then I want to go home."

"I think we need to get you cleared by Doc first," he said.

"How bad am I hurt?" Fable asked, as she tried to move. She cried out as a fiery pain shot through her shoulder and instantly stopped.

"Jesus Gypsy," Tripp said angrily. "Don't do that again." He carefully let her go and slid off the bed. Then he crossed the room and dragged a chair close to the bed. Once he was comfortable, he turned to her once more.

"Your shoulder actually wasn't hurt too bad. The knife went through and didn't hit anything major. Doc stitched it up and put it in a sling, telling me you'd have to wear it about three weeks. It's gonna hurt bad for a while, and you won't be able to use your arm, but you'll heal just fine," Tripp explained.

"And my hand?" Fable questioned, as she looked down at it. Tripp sighed.

"Your hand was hurt pretty bad. Because you're so fucking tiny, the knife did a lot of damage. It hit a couple small bones and tore through some muscle and tendons. Doc preformed surgery to repair what he could and bandaged it up. He said you'll need to wear a brace for about six weeks, then he'll let you know how it's healing." When he stopped, she knew that wasn't all.

"And?" she prompted.

"Your hand will never be as strong as it was, you'll have a bad scar, and you may have some issues with the feeling in some of your fingers."

"So," Fable said, as she thought about it. "I basically have no arms for the next month."

Tripp stared at her, and she could tell he wasn't sure how to answer.

"So, you'll have to help me with everything?" Fable asked. "You'll have to feed me, shower me and dress me?" she continued.

He still only stared at her, until she grinned, and he blinked in confusion.

"So, my big, badass, biker husband will have to wait on me hand and foot?" she giggled. "I'm so going to love this."

Finally, Tripp smirked, understanding that she wasn't going to flip out over this. "You have no idea how strong you are," he told her. "I've just told you some terrible news, and all you can think about is using me as your slave for the near seeable future."

"It could be fun," Fable grinned happily.

"Oh, I can make it fun," Tripp told her huskily.

"Hey," Steele called out, as he pushed open the door and poked his head in. "We heard voices. Is it safe to come in?"

"And the fun begins," Tripp replied sarcastically. Steele ignored him, and pushed the door all the way open, prowling into the room.

Fable lay on the bed, stunned as more and more bikers came through the door. When the room was completely full, she was blinking back tears. Not only had every biker in the club come to see her, but so had Mario and Darren.

"Oh my god," she cried. "I love you guys."

"No, you don't," Tripp growled from beside her. "Don't fucking tell them that."

"No take backs," Dagger yelled from his perch on the windowsill. "She loves us," he said in a sing song voice.

"Fucking Dagger," Tripp groaned in annoyance.

When Fable laughed, all the brothers turned to smile at her, and she knew no matter what happened with her injuries, it was worth it. The happiness she was experiencing with them, was something she never imagined she'd ever have.

Chapter 44
Tripp

The next day, Doc let Tripp take his girl home. He had stayed all night and was happy to see his Gypsy didn't have any nightmares. He was so proud of her for her high spirits. Yesterday the bikers had stayed for almost an hour, and Fable had laughed the whole time. When they left, most of them told him what a strong woman she was, and how happy they were to have her be a part of their club.

When Shadow left, she got a bit emotional. The brother had been the one to get the knife away from her neck and had saved her life. She had looked up at him gratefully and asked him to come close.

"I want to thank you for what you did," Fable whispered. "You saved my life."

But Shadow shook his head. "The club saved your life, I just helped."

She laughed. "Well, you were a big help."

"You're welcome honey," Shadow replied, then he kissed the top of her head. "I've got to go," he told them. "My woman wants to paint Preacher's room, and I really don't think he wants it painted. I've got to stop her before she starts a war," he explained. "Those two fight more than the brothers," he admitted, as he walked out the door.

"I love them," she told Tripp.

"I know Gypsy, just not too much," he ordered.

The next morning, he helped her dress, which was hard with her hand and shoulder, and brushed her hair. She had been upset about getting blood on the jeans he had bought her and figured they were ruined. Of course, that's when Doc came in. He explained that he got blood on his clothes all the time and the hospital had a special cleaner that got it out. He took her jeans and promised to see what he could do.

Doc ended up driving them back to the clubhouse, and she was thrilled they arrived in time for lunch. Tripp was surprised to see a group of brothers come in wearing tool belts and covered in saw dust. Apparently, Preacher was right, the brothers had gotten to work on his cabin as soon as they left. Tripp nodded at the brothers in thanks, and they nodded back.

Lunch had been sandwiches and fruit, so it hadn't been too hard to help Fable. Doc had given her more pain meds and then had wandered off. When Tripp saw she was getting tired, he took her back to his room. He loved how happy she was there.

"I'm gonna have to call my mom, but I don't know what to tell her," Fable sighed. "I really didn't tell her anything that was going on. I'm not sure how Gabe's dad will feel either."

"Give it a couple days, then we'll do it together. I'll come up with something," Tripp promised.

"Okay," Fable agreed, as she relaxed back on the colourful bed. It was then a knock came at the door. Tripp answered it, happy to see it was Sniper, Trike and Misty. Misty headed straight to the bed and plopped down beside Fable.

"How about you and me watch movies, and argue about who's husband's hotter?" Misty grinned.

"Oh, I like that," Fable replied, looking more alert.

Trike looked to the ceiling as he shook his head. "That's no argument," he huffed. "Everybody knows I win every time."

Tripp just laughed at the brother. "No girl wants a boy. They want a man," he smirked, as he pointed to himself.

"Your two fucking years older than me," Trike griped.

"All I have to do is put on my camo, strap my sniper rifle to my back, and I got you both beat," Sniper smirked as he headed out the door.

Both Tripp and Trike stared at the brothers back, then turned back to the girls. It looked like the two of them were drooling.

"If he weren't my brother, I'd pick him," Misty said giggling.

"Hey," Trike roared. "That's not funny."

"You own any camo?" Misty asked him.

"No, I wasn't in the military," Trike said in confusion.

"You own any camo?" Misty then asked Tripp.

"No, I was a cop," he answered.

"Oh," Misty exclaimed, as she bounced on the bed. "He has handcuffs and a uniform, he wins," she giggled.

"Fucking girls," Trike groaned, as he pushed Tripp out the door and slammed it shut. "Those two are trouble."

"Yep," Tripp agreed. "Is Misty there to look after Fable, while we end Gabe?" he questioned.

"Yep," Trike answered.

"Excellent," Tripp grinned, as he stomped down the hall eagerly.

Chapter 45
Tripp

Tripp followed Sniper and Trike out to the common room. Being a cop for so long, he'd heard rumours about the infamous shed, but that's all he thought it was. To find out it was real was a little intimidating. But if that's where Gabe was waiting for him, he was all for it.

Preacher was the first to greet him. "Brother," he said. "No cuts allowed in the shed. It can get pretty messy in there, and a cut's sacred. Take it off, fold it up, and store it behind the bar with the rest of the brother's," he ordered.

Tripp did as asked, and was surprised to see three other cuts already there. Trike and Sniper removed theirs as well and placed them beside his.

"Enjoy," Preacher encouraged, as he walked away and headed for his office.

Tripp followed his brothers out the door and was surprised to see they were headed out back behind the garage. Sitting in a spot just inside the tree line and hidden completely from view, was an actual shed. It was made out of wood, looked well used, and had a tinted window. Tripp walked over to the window and peered inside. It stunned him to find he couldn't see a thing.

"Did you actually think you'd be able to see in?" Trike snickered at him. "It lets in a bit of light, but it hides what's inside from curious fuckers," he explained. "We also made it soundproof, for obvious reasons."

"Of course," Tripp replied. The brothers headed for the door, and Snake opened it to allow the men inside.

Tripp blinked his eyes a couple times, until he got used to the dimmer light, then looked around. It honestly looked like a tool shed from the inside too. Tools lined the walls, and a work bench sat in the corner. The one thing that set it apart though, was the drain in the floor, and the brownish colour that stained the cement.

It was then he noticed Gabe. They had chained the goon to the ceiling, and he looked scared to death.

"How's he doing?" Tripp questioned.

"Well he hasn't pissed himself yet, so that's a plus," Navaho snickered. Tripp was surprised to see him, as well as Dragon and Steele inside. When he looked at Navaho in question, the huge biker just shrugged.

"Happens more than we'd like," Navaho explained. Then he moved to the far wall. "I built you something," he said, as he dragged a wooden platform towards the middle of the room. Dragon moved forward and helped him lay it down and slide it so it was flat on the floor directly under Gabe. Hooks were imbedded in each of the corners.

"Very inventive," Tripp told him appreciatively. "You put some thought into this."

"Yep," Navaho grinned. "I kind of figured this was the direction you would take, so I got a jumpstart on this."

Tripp walked around the platform, studying it for a few minutes. "It's perfect," he declared as he thanked the brother. "You got good instincts."

"I aim to please," Navaho chuckled.

"I know you're gonna kill me," Gabe cried. "Just put a fucking bullet in my head and get it over with."

Tripp stared at the brother angrily. "You stole my woman. You got rid of everyone and everything she loved. You took away her happiness and tried to break her. Then you staked her to the fucking floor with knives. You think a fucking bullet is the way I'm gonna go," he yelled.

"Yes," the ass cried, as the brothers laughed at him.

"Goon looks a little terrified," Dragon snickered as he watched him.

At those words, Gabe let loose and wet himself.

"Fucking every time," Navaho complained. Then he got out a hose and rinsed off the platform. "You couldn't fuck do that before I moved the platform."

"Not very considerate," Tripp agreed. He watched as Navaho put away the hose. "Strap the fucker down brothers," he ordered. "I'm ready to play."

Chapter 46
Tripp

Tripp stood back as Dragon unhooked the chains from the ceiling. Then he kicked the back of Gabe's knees, and the man fell hard onto the platform. Steele was there, and with a hard boot to the chest, the man found himself on his back. His arms were spread, and he was effectively chained to the hooks in the top corners of the platform.

Gabe struggled, but with the heavy chains, and all the brothers surrounding him, it was useless. Another set of chains were brought out, and his legs were spread and quickly secured. He was already stripped of everything but his pants, so Tripp could begin right away.

Steele approached Tripp with a leather tool roll and handed it to him. Tripp laid it on the platform close to the goon's head and away from the water, then untied it and rolled it out. Inside were a dozen pockets, and each pocket held a knife.

"Wow," Tripp acknowledged. "That's quite the collection."

Steele nodded. "I keep them really sharp."

Tripp pulled one out, and ran it along the bottom of Gabe's foot, slicing from his toes to his heel. "Nice", Tripp said, as the blood ran down onto the platform. Already Gabe was whining, so this was going to be aggravating.

"Grow some balls and die like a man," Tripp growled in annoyance.

"Cassie's husband did the same thing," Steele huffed. "He was a god damned pussy the minute we dragged him through the door," he told them. "Must be the whole abuse thing. They can hurt women, but they can't handle being hurt themselves."

Tripp agreed, but he only nodded, as he pulled out another knife. "I think I'll do your hand first, like you did to my Gypsy," he told Gabe. He moved close to the man's hand and held the knife above him.

"Now hold still," Tripp instructed, before slamming the knife down. The man's thumb was severed, and it rolled off the platform as he screamed in pain. "Shit I missed," Tripp said as he raised the knife again.

The next time he brought it down, the two middle fingers were severed. "Fuck, I'm terrible at this," he said, as he shook his head. The brothers chuckled from behind him. "Third times a charm," he grinned, as he brought the knife down and stuck it right into Gabe's palm. "Got it," he said proudly.

"You mother fucker," Gabe was yelling, while in pain. "I didn't cut off her fingers."

Tripp just shrugged as he grabbed another knife. Quickly this time, he slammed it into the man's other palm in one hard thrust. Gabe instantly stopped talking and started screaming again.

Over the next hour, they placed knives into the goon's ankles, arms, shoulders and legs. Anywhere the brothers figured would do damage, but not kill him. Finally, Gabe had lost it. He was barely screaming now, and he was sprouting gibberish. It was time to end him.

Tripp went for the longest knife in the set. Without a word, he turned and plunged it through Gabe's forehead. The man blinked twice, then his eyes closed. The fucker was dead.

Tripp wiped his hand on Gabe's pants, then stood and faced his brothers. "Thank you," he said sincerely. "Best thing I did was join this fucking club."

"We're proud to have you," Steele replied, as he slapped him on the back. "On the far side of the shed you'll find a couple outdoor showers. You've got a fresh set of clothes waiting for you there," Steele told him.

"When the fuck did you put in showers?" Trike questioned the man curiously.

"Navaho built them a couple days ago. He figures someone's gonna see us trouping through the compound covered in blood. We really don't want it to be one of the girls," Steele explained.

"Appreciated," Trike instantly replied.

"Shower, then join us in the common room for a shot of whiskey," Steele ordered.

"Sounds perfect," Tripp replied. Then he headed out the door and towards the back. It was finished, now all he needed was for his Gypsy to heal.

Chapter 47
Fable

Fable had fallen asleep while watching the movie. When she woke, the credits were rolling up. She blinked a couple times, then looked over to see Misty watching her. She smiled at her best friend.

"I didn't mean to fall asleep and miss the whole movie," Fable admitted.

Misty just giggled at her. "It was Pretty in Pink, I'm sure you've seen it a dozen times," she said.

Fable laughed too. "Probably," she admitted.

"Did you want to head out to the main room and see if the guys are there?" Misty asked.

Fable was noticing that Misty and Trike didn't like to be away from each other for very long. She completely understood because that was the way she felt about Tripp.

"Yes please," Fable replied happily.

Misty helped her off the bed, then fixed her hair for her. The two girls headed down the hall and into the common room. They found the men sitting around a table, and it looked like they were doing shots of whiskey. Both girls laughed as they headed their way.

"Gypsy," Tripp called out, when she got close.

She grinned at him and hurried to his side. He pushed his chair back and carefully pulled her down to sit on his lap.

"Did you rest?" he questioned, as he kissed her forehead.

"I did," Fable told him. "Missed over half the movie," she admitted. When she looked over at

Misty she smiled, seeing her friend was sitting on her husband's lap as well.

"You celebrating something?" she asked Tripp. "You seem really happy."

"I am," he told her. "My wife's safe, our cabin's being built, and our problems are over," he told her.

"Are they really?" Fable asked, hoping she caught onto his hidden meaning. He grinned at her.

"Funny thing," Sniper piped up, from across the table. "Gabe just packed up his things and disappeared. No one can find him, and it's been almost two days now."

Fable actually smiled, knowing exactly what Gabe's disappearance meant. "That's wonderful news," she said.

Suddenly Preacher pushed his chair back and stood, gaining everyone's attention.

"Fable honey, get your ass up here," he shouted. Fable wasn't too sure what was going on, but she stood with Tripp's help, and made her way over to him.

"You survived something horrible," Preacher declared. "And you did it while making jokes. You made this whole club god damned proud." Then he reached behind him and pulled out a leather vest. "Your vest was too damaged to repair, so I had a new one made. No member of this club goes around without a vest," he insisted.

Tears came to her eyes as he carefully slipped her hand through and pulled it up, gently laying it against her shoulder. When she looked up at him, he kissed her cheek.

"Hey," Tripp yelled from across the room. "You made her cry, then you kissed her. I don't care whether or not you're the prez, I'll fuck you up."

Preacher chuckled, then pushed her away. "You better go sooth his wounded ego," he told her.

She headed back to Tripp, to a loud round of applause. When she was close, he placed her back on his lap and kissed her senseless.

"Feel better now," Preacher laughed, but Tripp only gave him the finger. The prez shook his head and turned back to the group.

"Sniper, Raid, get your god damned asses up here," Preacher bellowed.

Both men looked at each and smiled, then pushed out their chairs and headed for Preacher. Steele stood as well and moved their way with two vests in his hand.

"You two fuckers make me proud. You've saved our asses several times, and we want you to be fully patched members. Get those prospect vests off, and get your new ones on," he ordered.

The brothers laughed as they did as they were told. "Welcome to The Stone Knight's boys", Preacher roared, and the sound of the cheers in the room was deafening.

Tripp kissed her again. "Are you happy?" he asked.

"More than happy," she told him. Then she kissed him again just because she could.

Epilogue

Two weeks later, Tripp and Fable had moved into their cabin. They did it up in a mellower version of their room. Bright, comfy furniture filled it, patterned rugs covered the floors, and material covered lamps gave off light. Even Tripp admired the effect of all the colours. It suited his Gypsy so much, he couldn't argue.

Fable's shoulder was healing well and was beginning to itch. She was having a terrible time though since she couldn't itch it herself. She was getting a bit of feeling back in her fingers too. Doc was flabbergasted as he had believed that would never happen. Fable just smiled and went on as if she never had a doubt. His girl always amazed him.

They also found out from Doc, that the real estate agent, Tara, was doing better. The knife hadn't hit anything major, but she would be experiencing a lot of back pain on and off in the future, and may end up in a wheelchair in the future. Overall, she was extremely lucky, it could have been worse.

Fable had finally broken down and called her mother. The call was put on speaker, so Gabe's dad had listened in. She had been afraid about talking to him, but he turned out to be incredibly nice. She explained about how Gabe had made her break up with Tripp, and how he was after her settlement. They left out the part about him killing Kevin; it wasn't something they could ever prove anyway.

They then explained that they were married, and that they had made Tripp her beneficiary. Her mother had been disappointed that she missed the wedding, but was thrilled that Tripp and her were back together. When they explained that Gabe had disappeared, his father said it was for the best. Gabe had been a difficult son at the best of times.

They hung up on good terms, with promises to visit soon. Fable had decided not to tell them about her injuries, her shoulder would be healed when they came, and they could come up with something about her hand.

Two days later a package arrived at the front gates. Fable had been shocked to find it was from her mother. When Tripp opened it for her, she had cried. Inside was her father's old mining helmet. When Tripp pulled it out and flipped it over, they found a picture of her dad and a young Fable inside. Her father had taped the picture of them to the inside of his helmet and carried it with him at work.

When Navaho found out about it, he made a special case for the helmet, and they placed it on the fireplace. Misty copied the picture and blew it up, and they framed it and placed it beside the helmet.

A couple days after moving in, Fable had her birthday. She saw the lawyer and signed all the paperwork, then left with a huge cheque in her hand. They went straight to the bank and deposited it, deciding that they would put most in a trust for any kids they had.

Misty now had her photography business back to where she wanted it, so Fable spent her days helping her. Tripp helped out at the garage, but he spent most of his time gathering information and helping out the club and Mario. His detective skills and his know how on the ins and outs of the law, was making him a huge asset to both.

His captain even came by to offer him his job back, but Tripp refused. He was extremely happy with his new life, and he wasn't changing anything. Fable was his wife now, they were trying for a baby, and he had a huge new family. There wasn't anything else he needed.

About the Author

MEGAN FALL is a mother of three who helps her husband run his construction business. She has been writing all her life, but with a push from her daughter, started publishing. It's the best thing she ever did. When she's not writing, you can find her at the beach. She loves searching for rocks, sea glass, driftwood and fossils. She believes in ghosts, collects ridiculous amounts of plants, and rides on the back of her hubby's motorcycle.

MEGAN FALL

Look for these books coming soon!

STONE KNIGHTS MC SERIES

Finding Ali
Saving Cassie
Loving Misty
Rescuing Tiffany
Guarding Alexandria
Protecting Fable
Surviving November
Sheltering Macy
Defending Zoe

DEVILS SOLDIERS MC SERIES

Resisting Diesel
Surviving Hawk

THE ENFORCER SERIES

The Enforcer
The Enforcers Revenge

Surviving November
Stone Knight's Book 7

Chapter One
Jude

Jude stared at the moving truck as it pulled into the driveway next door. He had heard someone had bought the house, but it had been vacant so long, he had given up hope that anybody would want it. It was a pretty little house, but it needed a ton of work. He pitied the person that had decided to take on that project.

When the truck stopped, two large guys stepped out and moved to the back, pulling up the rolling door. Jude watched for hours as piece after piece of flowery furniture was carried into the small house. Fascinated, he couldn't wait to see what crazy person was moving in.

In hours they were done, and the rolling door was pulled down, then the men were climbing back in the truck and driving away. Jude had washed his Harley and cut the grass, in the time it had taken to empty the truck. When no one else came or went, he gave up watching. Climbing on his bike, he headed out to run the few errands he needed to do.

The grocery store was first. He ate out tons, so he pretty much only needed snacks. Even he'd admit, he was a good cook, but because he only cooked for himself, he rarely bothered. His next stop was to the beer store, he was usually on his Harley, so it was impossible to cart the cases home. What he did, was pay one of the stock boys to deliver it after his shift, it worked out well for both of them. The kid made a couple bucks, and Jude didn't have to take his truck to cart the beer home.

An hour later he was back. He unpacked the small amount of groceries he had bought, then headed outside when he heard the roar of a motorcycle. Glancing up, he saw Navaho headed his way. The biker pulled into his driveway, turned off his Harley, and climbed off.

Navaho was a member of The Stone Knight's, the local biker club. They were all decent men, and Jude hung out with them a lot. They were bugging him to prospect, but Jude wasn't sure he'd fit in. Most of the guys were honest, hard-working men, some were even military men, but Jude had done prison time.

He didn't want to bring that kind of bad to a club that was respected.

Jude greeted Navaho with a grin and a half hug. The man didn't talk much, but he was good company. Navaho took a seat on one of the two chairs on the porch while Jude went in for a six pack. Once it was on the porch between them, and they each had a cold one, they shot the shit.

A couple hours later, a sleek black car pulled up to the curb in front of the house next door. An old blue clunker, that sounded like it would backfire and take out the block, pulled into the drive. A big man in a suit got out of the fancy black car, while a tiny pixie, with long dark hair and glasses, got out of the clunker. She had her hands on her hips, and her head tilted to the side, as she studied the small house.

"Hmmm," Navaho said in surprise. "Someone finally had the guts to buy that shit hole," he said, as he watched the scene unfolding in front of him. Jude knew they couldn't be seen, as huge evergreen shrubs surrounded his porch.

"Guess so," Jude replied. "Moving truck came today, flowery shit went in, then the moving truck left. If that idiots moving in with her, he's either gay, or he's whipped," he chuckled. Navaho snickered beside him.

The couple chatted for a minute, then the man hugged the pixie, kissed her on the head, then ruffled her dark curls. She fumed as she tried to swat him, but missed and fell flat on her ass. The man sighed, then helped her up and attempted to dust her off. That didn't go over so well as she kicked him in the shin. Navaho chuckled again beside him.

"Guess they're not a couple," he commented.

The man headed for his car, and the woman turned and headed for the steps. She tripped on the first one, but caught herself on the railing before she fell again. The man was already turning to head back, but she waved him off.

"Christ she's a klutz," Jude groaned, and Navaho nodded.

"You're gonna have to keep on eye on that one. She's likely to burn down the house, and take out yours with it," Navaho told him seriously.

"Fuck off," Jude huffed in annoyance. Then they watched as the man drove off, and the woman disappeared into the house.

Little did Jude know, that tiny pixie was about to become a huge pain in the ass.

Made in the USA
Monee, IL
17 December 2023

49624534R00142